SCREENPLAY BY

Kevin Smith

talk miramax books

HYPERION

NEW YORK

ISBN: 0-7868-8762-1

First Edition

10 9 8 7 6 5 4 3 2 1

This book is dedicated to my wife, Jennifer.

Now, many of you will assume I *have* to do that, because she's my wife, and if I want to continue getting laid, I'll dedicate a book (hell, *every* book) to her. However, this is not the case (though I *do* want to continue getting laid).

I dedicate this book to Jen because *Jay and Silent Bob Strike Back* monopolized our second year of marriage—just as *Dogmas* monopolized our first year of marriage. In truth, I imagine there will be films and movies and comics and whatnot monopolizing every year of our marriage. And my hope is that Jen will afford me as much space and patience and support on the future projects as she has on this one—the one with the shameless marketing tie-in you're now holding.

So, if you'll indulge me, I'd like to share a few private thoughts with my wife. Please turn the page, now, if you're not her.

ahem

Jenny, I love you. You're more wife than I ever deserved, and more woman than this wannabe-man can sometimes handle. You've sacrificed countless hours of precious time we could've spent loving each other so that I might tell stories about a guy who runs around trying to fuck anything that moves while screaming "Snoogans!" indiscriminately at the top of his lungs. And though it pays our bills, so, too, would a normal nine-to-five job. And while the former takes me away from you too often, the latter would allow for far more intimate one-on-one time between a couple who only just met three years ago and are still trying to unravel the mysteries of each other.

However, even knowing all that, you've never once said, "Quit your multi-million-dollar-a-year earning gig and go back to work at the Quick Stop so that we can have our weekends free."

And for that, I cherish you.

Thank you, Boo. Thanks for understanding. I owe you.

This script is a lousy read.

Seriously—I just scanned through the mess, prior to sending it off to Talk Miramax for publishing, and it just lies there on the page. The jokes are flat, the plot is . . . well, insipid, and the characterizations are two-dimensional at best. In short, gentle reader, if you've just plunked down some hard-earned cash for this tome, you were screwed.

However, I say all that after having lived with the actual movie for the last four months.

The movie, *Jay and Silent Bob Strike Back,* is far, far better than the script for *Jay and Silent Bob Strike Back,* inasmuch as it lives and breathes as this great, vulgar beast with a smart-alecky grin that dares you *not* to laugh—all while wearing its heart on its snot-stained sleeve.

In retrospect, that should've been the tag line on the poster.

So, why is it that the movie's a "wacky and rollicking thrill ride" (I borrowed that from a critical blurb in the ad for *Josie and the Pussycats*) while the script is merely "shit, pure shit" (my mom's review of the script)? Well, it's because of the talented artisans responsible for fleshing out the words you're about to read who really make the movie . . . well, move. Everyone from Affleck (who lent his usual charming and devilish wit to the proceedings), to Mosier (my *real* hetero lifemate and producer extraordinaire), to Keith (the key set production assistant who, on more than one occasion, secured for me a peanut butter and jelly sandwich) *made* this movie. Without them and the hundreds of others—cast *and* crew—who pulled together to bring this sorry story to life, *Jay and Silent Bob Strike Back* is merely the scribblings of a guy who apparently loves the "f" word an awful lot.

However, above all else, there was one person without whom this movie never rises above the page.

Jason Mewes.

I can wax poetical about Mewes for thirty pages, enlightening you as to just how integral he was to not just this movie, but *every* movie View

Askew has thus far had a hand in producing (well, except *Good Will Hunt-ing*; although I can make a viable argument that Mewes in the Affleck role might've pushed the grosses on that wildly successful flick into *Titanic* territory). But for proof of the genius of Jay, I need only to point you to any page of this book that contains dialogue. Flip to, oh, let's say page twenty-six and read it. Go ahead. I'll wait . . .

Okay, now what did you read? A random selection of profanity that you can find on any public restroom stall wall, right? But for some reason, when it's coming out of Mewes's mouth, it's never just that. Those words, when recited—or rather, *performed*—by Mewes, are elevated beyond the gutter and delivered into the sublime. Yes, the sheer audacity of the com-ments are there on the sterile page; but it's the heart of Mewes himself that transforms them from simple, potty-mouth expressions into the vocal-ized *id* of the luckiest character in the world, fictional or otherwise: the person who gets to say what's on his mind because what's on his mind *isn't* on his mind very long before it comes blasting out of his mouth.

We live guarded lives in a world where truth is rarely encouraged, and empty pleasantries are the favored manner of non-communication. Don't believe me? Go turn on any late-night talk show and listen to the vapid exchanges. Now turn the volume down and imagine what the interviewer and the interviewee would *really* be saying, were they not trying to sell something—be it movie or image. Ah, the ratings boost late-night would see if guest after guest actually had the balls to tell Leno to go fuck him-self.

The beauty of the Jay character, and the reason, I suspect, he's con-nected so well with audiences the world over is that Jay is incapable of empty pleasantries. He *would* tell Leno to go fuck himself. Jay says what he's thinking, often before he's finished thinking it. He doesn't weigh his words carefully, nor does he think (or know) that he *should,* in order to fit in with the world around him. He just speaks. At great lengths. Usually about getting laid. And you're kidding yourself if you think that's not what *everyone in the world* would choose to talk about if social propriety, image consciousness, and accountability weren't the orders of the day.

Very few actors can get away with playing that character, which speaks volumes on the Mewes appeal. There's a sweetness about Jason that in-forms the character of Jay, so much so that he can speak sincerely, and straight-faced, about fucking you in your ass—and you're not disgusted or alarmed enough to call a cop. In fact, you find yourself entertaining the notion—even if you're a guy. And my guess is it's because Mewes—like Jay—is a man filled with conviction, no matter how misguided. And there are very few men of that ilk around anymore.

I say this with the utmost sincerity: Jason Mewes is the finest actor I have ever worked with or beside. And I know this because most of the people who've seen the *Jersey Chronicles* believe he's *not* acting when he's playing Jay; they assume that's what Mewes is really like. And he's content to allow people to assume that, because he lacks ego.

And because, if it's going to get him laid, why ruin a good thing?

So my backwards cap is off to Jason Mewes. Without him, the words in this book are a stunningly misspelled and gramatically atrocious collection of profane non sequiturs.

Because of him, though, they're magic.

Snoogans, Mister Mewes.

Snoogans, indeed.

Kevin Smith
July 13, 2001

OVER BLACK WE SEE:

CHYRON

A long time ago, in front of a convenience store far, far away . . .

EXT. QUICK STOP YEARS AGO—DAY

We FADE IN *on the block of stores (Quick Stop/RST), from some time ago. In fact, RST isn't RST; it's* THE RECORD RACK—*a 45's store with head shop paraphernalia in the window. A white-trash* MOTHER *(maybe seventeen) wearing a baseball cap comes into frame carrying a chubby* BABY. *The Baby wears an oversized t-shirt under what looks like a little bathrobe, and messily eats a* CHOCOLATE BAR. *There are food stamps in the Mother's hands.*

MOTHER

Bobby-Boy stay here while mommy picks up the free cheese, 'kay?

She looks up at the bright sun, shielding her eyes slightly, then looks back at the baby on the ground. She takes off her baseball cap and places it on the baby.

MOTHER

This'll keep the sun out of your eyes. You be good now.

She walks away, leaving the baby sitting against the wall. With the backwards baseball cap and the chocolate around his mouth forming something that resembles a beard, the kid looks kind of familiar.

Then, another MOTHER *(also very young) decked out in a* KISS *concert shirt from years gone by and huge, feathered hair enters, with a black skullcap wearing* BABY *slung at her hip. She sees the first Baby sitting against the wall and sets her Baby down beside him.*

MOTHER

Don't fucking move, you little shit-machine. Mommy's gonna try to score.

A PASSERBY *enters, heading toward the convenience store. He takes note of the Babies and the Mother heading into the record store, and then stops and addresses her, disgusted.*

PASSERBY

Excuse me—who's watching these babies?

MOTHER

The fat one's watching the little one.

PASSERBY

Oh, nice parenting.
(walking away)
Leave 'em out here like that and see what happens.

The Passerby walks away. The Mother flips him the bird.

MOTHER

FUCK YOU, YOU FUCKING SQUARE!

PASSERBY

(waving her off)
Ah, keep on truckin'.

MOTHER

(to baby)
D'jou hear that crazy fuck tellin' me how to fuckin' raise you? Motherfucker, man! Who's he fucking think he is? What's the worse fuckin' thing could happen to you sitting outside the fuckin' stores? Fuck!

The door closes, and the Babies sit there quietly for a beat. Then, they look at each other. The larger one says nothing. The smaller one says . . .

BABY

Fuck, fuck, fuck . . .

DISSOLVE TO:
THE PRESENT

JAY *and* SILENT BOB *stand where the Babies sat. The Record Rack is now RST VIDEO. Jay is mid-chant.*

> ### JAY
> *(as a chant)*
> . . . fuck, fuck, fuck, mother-mother fuck, mother-mother fuck-fuck! Mother-fuck, mother-fuck, noinch-noinch-noinch-noinch!
> *(counting off; singing)*
> One, two, one, two, three, four! Noinch, noinch, noinch, smoking weed, smoking weed, doing coke, drinking beers! Drinking beers, beers, beers, rolling fatties, smoking blunts! Who smokes the blunts? We smoke the blunts!

A pair of TEENS *approach them.*

> ### TEEN 1
> Lemme get a nickel bag.

> ### JAY
> Fifteen bucks, little man. Put the money in my hand. If the money does not show, then you owe-me-owe-me-owe.
> *(changing up to Morris Day)*
> *My Jungle Love! Yes! Oh-we-oh-we-oh! I think I want to know ya', know ya'* . . .

> ### TEEN 1
> *(digging in pockets)*
> What the hell are you singing?

> ### JAY
> You don't know "Jungle Love"? That shit is the mad notes. Written by God Herself and handed down to the world's greatest band—the motherfucking Time.

> ### TEEN 2
> The guys in that Prince movie?

> ### TEEN 1
> *Purple Rain.*

TEEN 2

Man, that shit was so gay—fucking eighties style.

Jay suddenly grabs the kid by the throat, throwing him against the wall.

JAY

Bitch, don't you *NEVER* say an unkind word about The Time!
Me and Silent Bob modeled our whole fucking *lives* after Morris
Day and Jerome! I'm a smooth pimp who loves the pussy, and
Tubby here's my black manservant!

Just then, RANDAL exits the video store, locking the door behind him.

RANDAL

What'd I tell you two about dealing in front of the store? Drop
the kid and peddle your wares someplace else, burn-boy.
(*walking away*)
And for the record, The Time sucked ass.

He exits. Jay, Silent Bob, and the Teens watch him go. After a beat . . .

JAY

Yo—youse guys wanna hear something fucked up about him and
the Quick Stop guy?

INT. QUICK STOP—DAY

*Randal joins DANTE behind the counter. Dante rings up a customer, a
half-eaten submarine sandwich sitting on the counter. Randal grabs it,
takes a bite, and starts reading a newspaper.*

RANDAL

Hey, can't we do something about those two stoners hanging
around outside all the time?

DANTE

Why? What'd they do now?

RANDAL

I'm trying to watch *Clash of the Titans*, and all I can hear is the
two of them screaming about Morris Day at the top of their lungs.

DANTE

I thought the fat one didn't really talk much.

RANDAL

What, am I producing an *A&E Biography* about 'em? I'm just saying they shouldn't be loitering around the stores like they do.

DANTE

Neither should *you*, but we let *you* stay.

RANDAL

See, man—if you were funnier than that, ABC never would've cancelled us.

DANTE

What?

RANDAL

Nothing.

Enter Teen 1 and Teen 2, chuckling.

TEEN 1

Two packs of Wraps.
                              (beat)
Yo—how was the service?

RANDAL

What service?

TEEN 2

The one at the Unitarian Church where you two got married to each other last week.

RANDAL

What the hell are you talking about?

TEEN 1

Jay said you had a *Star Wars*–themed wedding and you guys tied the knot dressed like storm troopers.

TEEN 2

Yeah. And he said you're the bitch and you're the butch. Oh, sorry—the Leia and the Luke.

DANTE

I'm the bitch?!

RANDAL
Well if we *were* gay, that's how I'd see it.

DANTE
Would you shut up?!

TEEN 1
(to Teen 2)
Holy shit, dude. The honeymoon's over.

DANTE
We're not married to each other.

TEEN 1
Well, sure. Not in the eyes of the state or any real church,
Skywalker.

RANDAL
(heading for the phone)
That does it. I'm gonna do something about those two I shoulda
done a long time ago . . .

TEEN 2
In a galaxy far, far away!

TEEN 1
(exiting)
May the Foreskin be with you, Hand-Jabba the Hutt.

RANDAL
(into phone)
Yeah, I want to report a couple of drug dealers out in front of the
Quick Stop.

EXT. QUICK STOP—DAY

*Jay and Silent Bob are thrown against the wall outside by a COP, who
frisks them and checks their pockets.*

JAY
What the fuck, Serpico?! What'd we do?

COP

We got a report that two guys were hanging around outside the stores, selling pot.

JAY

We don't smoke pot, yo.

Teen 1 enters and hands Jay rolling papers.

TEEN 1

Here're the rolling papers you wanted for your pot. And your change. Thanks.
                    (getting in Jay's face)
And The Time sucks ass.

Teen 1 races off. Jay and Bob move to follow, but the Cop stops them, grabbing the rolling papers out of Jay's hand. He eyeballs the pair.

COP

No pot, hunh? What do you need *this* for?

JAY

What? I got a wiping problem. I stick these little pieces of paper over my brown-eye, and bam—no shit stains in my undies.
                    (unbuttoning pants)
You don't believe me? Lemme show you.

Jay drops his pants and leans against the wall, looking back over his shoulder.

JAY

Just spread my cheeks a little, and you can see the fucking stink nuggets . . .

COP

Pull up your pants up, sir. Now!

Jay bends down to pull up his pants and FARTS. *Silent Bob cracks up. The Cop grabs them both, leading them toward the car.*

COP

Let's take a ride down to the station.

JAY

What? It's suddenly a crime to fart, motherfucker?!

EXT. BRODIE BRUCE'S SECRET STASH COMIC BOOK STORE—DAY

An ESTABLISHING SHOT *of Brodie's store in the heart of Red Bank.*

BRODIE (O.C.)

No fucking way!

WE GO TIGHT *on the huge, cartoon sign of* BRODIE *outside to . . .*

INT. BRODIE BRUCE'S SECRET STASH COMIC BOOK STORE—LATER

. . . BRODIE *himself, holding a stack of comics in one hand and a Dixie cup in the other. Jay and Silent Bob follow him as he puts new books in the racks.*

BRODIE

Dante and Randal slapped you with a restraining order?!

JAY

Judge said if we go within within a hundred feet of the stores, we get thrown into County.

BRODIE

So you gonna abide by the court's ruling or you gonna go *Bandit*—Reynolds style?

JAY

Fuck yeah! You know what they make you do in County? Toss the fucking salad! I don't lick *this* fuck's asshole; I'm gonna do it for some stranger?

BRODIE

I guess if you really wanted to hang out in front of a convenience store, you could just buy your own now—what with all that money you guys made.

JAY

Hell yeah, bitch.

(beat)

Wait a second—what money?

                              BRODIE
        The money from the movie, dumb-ass.

                               JAY
        What the fuck are you babbling about?

                              BRODIE
        (pulling a bagged-and-boarded issue down from the wall)
        The *Bluntman and Chronic* movie.
                           (dawns on him)
        Oh my God—don't tell me you have no idea there's a movie
        being made of the comic you two were the basis for.

                               JAY
        What?! Since when?

                              BRODIE
        Goddamit, man . . .
                          (taps his wrist)
        Here's the pulse, alright. And here's your finger . . .
                  (shoves his hand down the back of his pants)
        . . . far from the pulse, jammed straight up your ass.
                   (extracts hand and extends it to Jay)
        Say—would you like a chocolate-covered pretzel?

Brodie leads them back to the counter.

                              BRODIE
        You see, kids, if you read *Wizard*, you'd know it's the top story
        this month. Check it out.

Brodie hands Jay and Silent Bob a copy of Wizard, *opened to the headline:*
Snootchie Bootchies! Bluntman and Chronic Get Big Screen Treatment!
There are pictures of HOLDEN MCNEIL *and* BANKY EDWARDS, *as*
well as drawings of Bluntman and Chronic.

                               JAY
        When the fuck did this happen?!

                              BRODIE
        Well, after *X-Men* hit at the box office, all the studios started
        buying up every comic property they could get their hands on.
        Miramax optioned *Bluntman and Chronic*.

JAY

Miramax? I thought they only made classy flicks like *The Piano* and *The Crying Game?*

BRODIE

Yeah, well once they made *She's All That*, everything went to hell. So you're saying you *haven't* gotten a cut of the movie? Didn't Holden McNeil and Banky Edwards used to pay you likeness rights for the comic book?

JAY

We haven't seen a fucking dime for no movie!

BRODIE

Well boys, I'm no lawyer, but I think Holden and Banky owe you some of that proverbial phat cash. I mean, they're making a movie based on characters that are based on you and Quiet Robert.

JAY

It ain't me and Quiet Robert. It's a pair of stupid-ass superheroes that run around saying "Snitchy-Nitchies" or something.

BRODIE

I believe it's "Snootchie Boochies." Regardless—you're getting screwed. If I was you guys I'd confront Holden McNeil and ask him for my movie check.

JAY

Shit yeah. We gotsta get paid.

BRODIE

And on that note, we cue the music.

Jay lays down a House bass beat. Brodie complements it with his own beat.

EXT. POTZER'S INC—DAY

Jay and Silent Bob mosey past the front door of the building and knock.

INT. POTZER'S INC—DAY

HOLDEN McNEIL *opens the door and smiles.*

HOLDEN

Well! I have been waiting years to do this.
                    (smiles)
Look at these morose motherfuckers right here. Smells like
someone shit in their cereal. Bunngg!

Jay and Silent Bob enter. Holden closes the door, following them.

JAY

What the fuck took you so long answering your damn door? You
trying to talk *another* girlfriend of yours into some of that gay-
ass three-way action with your buddy?

HOLDEN

No, I was just showering your mother's stink off me after I gave
her a quick jump and sent her home. But now that you mention
it . . .
                    (to Bob)
Thanks, you know. You could've made the moral of that story
you told me a *bit* more clear.

Silent Bob shrugs.

HOLDEN

So what brings you two dirt merchants to my neck of the woods?

JAY

Oh, I'll tell you what our necks are doing in your woods . . .

Silent Bob holds up the Wizard *article.*

JAY

Where's our motherfucking movie check?!

HOLDEN

You heard about that too, hunh? Well, I've got nothing to do with
it. That's Banky's deal. He owns the property now. I signed my
half of the *Bluntman and Chronic* rights over to him years ago.

JAY

Why the fuck would you do a thing like that?

HOLDEN

Because I'm almost thirty, for God's sake—why on earth would
I want to keep writing about characters whose central preoccupa-
tions are weed and dick and fart jokes? You gotta grow, man.
Don't *you* ever want more for yourself?
(off Silent Bob)
I *know* this poor, hapless sonovabitch does. I look in his doe eyes
and I see a man crying out, "When, Lord? When the fuck can
your servant ditch this foul-mouthed little chucklehead to whom
I am a constant victim of his folly, and who bombards me and
those around us with grade-A foolishness that prevents me from
even getting to kiss a girl? Fuck! When?!"

*Silent Bob nods like he's finally understood. Jay looks at him, hurt, and
Bob tries to downplay the comment's truth.*

JAY

I'm the chucklehead? Fuck you—you're the dumb-ass who gave
away his comic, and now you ain't got no fat movie check neither.

HOLDEN

When you're right, you're right. I wish I'd broken off a little piece
for myself. Because if the buzz is any indication, the movie's
gonna make some huge bank.

JAY

What buzz?

HOLDEN

The Internet buzz.

JAY

What the fuck is the Internet?

INT. OFFICE OF POTZERS INC.—LATER

*Holden's at a computer terminal. Jay and Silent Bob look over his
shoulder.*

HOLDEN

The Internet is a communication device that allows people the
world over to bitch about movies and share pornography with one
another.
(off monitor)
Here's what we're looking for: 'Movie PoopShoot.com.'

JAY
(to Bob)
"Poop Chute." Yeaaahhh.

HOLDEN
This is a site full of militant movie buffs: sad bastards who live
in their parents' basements, downloading scripts and trading what
they believe to be inside info about movies and actors they
despise yet can't stop discussing. This is where you go if you
wanna hear frustrated would-be filmmakers mouth off with their
two-bit, arm-chair-director's opinions on how they all could've
made a better *Episode One*.

*On the computer monitor, we see the site mainpage load up. Holden
begins navigating the site.*

HOLDEN
Here. This is about the *Bluntman* movie.
(reading)
"Inside sources tell me Miramax is starting production this Friday
on their adaptation of underground comic fave *Bluntman and
Chronic*."

JAY
Friday?! Shit. Does it say who's playing us in the movie?

HOLDEN
No, but if it's Miramax, I'm sure it'll be Ben Affleck and Matt
Damon. They put 'em in a bunch of movies.

JAY
Who?

HOLDEN
You know—the guys from *Good Will Hunting*.

JAY
You mean that fucking movie with Mork from Ork in it?

HOLDEN
Yeah, I'm not too big a fan either. Though Affleck *was* the bomb
in *Phantoms*.

JAY

Word, bitch. *Phantoms* like a motherfucker.

Holden and Jay slap hands. Holden points at the monitor again.

HOLDEN

Now down here is where you can gauge the buzz. This is the
Shoot Back area. It's where people who read the news get to
chime in with their two cents. Here's what a guy who goes by the
chick-magnet Net handle of "Wampa-One" thinks about
Bluntman and Chronic.
(reading)
"Bluntman and Chronic and their stupid alter egos Jay and Silent
Bob only work in small doses, if at all. They don't deserve their
own movie."
(to Jay)
He's got a point.

JAY

Fuck him. What's the next one say?

HOLDEN
(reading)
"*Bluntman and Chronic* is the worst comic I ever read. Jay and
Silent Bob are stupid characters. A couple of stoners who spout
dumb-ass catchphrases like a third-rate Cheech and Chong or Bill
and Ted. Fuck Jay and Silent Bob. Fuck them up their stupid
asses."

JAY

Who the fuck said *that* shit?!

HOLDEN

A guy who calls himself "Magnolia-Fan." Check out what the
guy after him said: "Jay and Silent Bob are terrible, one-note
jokes that only stoners laugh at. They're fucking clown shoes. If
they were real, I'd beat the shit out of them for being so stupid. I
can't believe Miramax would have anything to do with this shit.
I, for one, will be boycotting this movie. Who's with me?"
(leans back)
And then there are about fifty more posts from people who agree
to join Spartacus-here's boycott of the flick.

JAY
(grimly)
I'm gonna kill all these fucks . . .

HOLDEN
Ah, let it go. Number one, they're a bunch of jealous little dicks who use the anonymity of the Net to insult people who're doing what they wish *they* were doing, and number two, they're not really talking about *you* guys—they're talking about Bluntman and Chronic.

JAY
But they said *Jay and Silent Bob!* They used our *real* names. It doesn't matter that there's a comic book version of us and a *real* version, 'cause nobody knows we're *real* in real life.

HOLDEN
Really.

JAY
Yeah! And all these people who read that shit think the *real* Jay and Silent Bob are a couple of faggots 'cause of what all these dicks are writing about the *comic book* Jay and Silent Bob! And maybe one night, me and Lunchbox'll be macking some bitch, and she'll be like "Oooo! I want to suck youse guys's dicks off. What's your names?" And I'll be like, "Jay and Silent Bob." And she'll be like, "Oh—I read on the Internet that youse guys were little fucking jerkoffs." And then she goes and sucks two *other* guys's dicks off instead! Well fuck that! We gotta put a *stop* to these hateful sonsa-bitches before they ruin our good names!

HOLDEN
First off, I don't know how good your names really are. Secondly, there's not much you can do about stopping this bile. The Internet's given everyone in America a voice, and everyone in America has chosen to use that voice to bitch about movies. As long as there's a *Bluntman and Chronic* movie, the Net-nerds are gonna have something negative to say about it.

Jay steams, thinking. Then, a light dawns on him.

JAY
But wait a second—if there *wasn't* a *Bluntman and Chronic*

movie, then no one would be saying shit about Jay and Silent Bob, right?

HOLDEN
They're not saying anything about you now—they're talking about fictional characters!

JAY
(oblivious to Holden; to Bob)
So all we gotta do is stop 'em from making the movie!

HOLDEN
Yeah, and kiss off the hundreds of thousands of dollars in royalties you're due in the process. Are you fucking retarded? Look, I'm probably not alone in the opinion that this flick is the worst idea since Greedo shooting first. I mean, a Jay and Silent Bob movie? Who would pay to see that?

Holden, Jay, and Silent Bob pause and look at the camera for a beat. Then . . .

HOLDEN
But since it *is* happening, you might as well just ignore the idiots on the Internet, go find Banky, and get your "motherfucking movie check," as you so succinctly put it. That's what's important here.

JAY
No, Holden McNeil—what's important here is that there's a bunch of motherfuckers we don't even know calling us assholes on the Internet to a bunch of teenagers and guys who can't even get laid. Putting a stop to that is the most important thing we could ever do.
(off monitor)
When did it say they're making that movie?

HOLDEN
They start this Friday.

JAY
So if today's Tuesday, that gives us . . .
(counts)
Eight days.

                    HOLDEN
It's more like three days.

                    JAY
Right. Three days to stop that stupid fucking movie from getting
made! C'mon, Silent Bob . . .

Jay and Bob stand and look at each other, filled with purpose.

                    JAY
We're going to Hollywood.

They stride off. Holden shakes his head.

                    HOLDEN
Now that's what I call the Blunt leading the Blunt.

EXT. BUS STATION—DAY

*Jay and Silent Bob approach a bus that's labeled "Los Angeles." They
nod at each other and then climb aboard. After a beat, they re-emerge.*

                    JAY
Tickets? Since when did they start charging for the bus?

They head toward the depot.

                    JAY
Didn't we used to ride that shit to school every day for free?

EXT. HIGHWAY—DAY

The bus roars past a sign that reads: Leaving New Jersey.

INT. BUS—SAME

Jay makes his way up to the DRIVER.

                    JAY
We in Hollywood yet?

                    DRIVER
It's a three-day ride to Los Angeles, sir. We left twenty minutes
ago.

JAY

I didn't aks you about Los Angeles. I aksed you about Hollywood.

DRIVER

Hollywood's *in* Los Angeles, sir.

JAY

Don't change the subject! Are we in Hollywood yet or not?

DRIVER

Please sit down, sir.

Jay glares at the Driver and heads back to his seat.

JAY

Why don't you take *your* seat, Ralph Kramden . . .

Jay slumps into the seat beside Silent Bob.

JAY

I'm fucking bored, man. There ain't shit to do on this bus.

Silent Bob mimes jerking off.

JAY

I already did that. Twice.

Silent Bob shrugs, looking out the window. Jay looks across the aisle and spots a CHILD IN A HELMET *playing a handheld video game. He leans over to him.*

JAY

Yo, Gretzsky—lemme get a turn.

CHILD

Leave me alone, little kid.

The Child gives him the finger. Jay goes wide-eyed, turning to Silent Bob.

JAY

That fuck called me a little kid and gave me the finger! Go kick his ass!

Silent Bob offers an incredulous look, as if to say, "He's ten years old."

JAY

You're my muscle, ain'tcha?

Silent Bob kind of nods.

JAY

So go open a can of whup-ass on that little fuck, and get me his
game!

*Silent Bob sighs and stands. He climbs over Jay into the aisle and stands
in front of the Child. He looks at him and registers doubt. He looks back
to Jay, who waves him on. Silent Bob steels himself, looks back to the kid
and reaches for his game. The Child emits a high-pitched scream and
starts punching himself in the head. Silent Bob dives back into his seat,
trying to look nonchalant. The Child stops crying. Jay looks at Silent Bob.*

JAY

You're one tough motherfucker, you know that?

EXT. HIGHWAY—DAY

The bus pulls over by the side of the road.

INT. BUS—DAY

*The Bus Driver heads down the aisle toward the back of the bus, followed
by pissed-off PASSENGERS.*

PASSENGER

They been in there going on half an hour now! Two of them!
Doing God knows what!

The Bus Driver bangs on the bathroom door and shouts.

DRIVER

This bus isn't moving another inch unless you clear out of there
right now!

No answer. The Bus Driver bangs on the door harder.

DRIVER
DO YOU HEAR ME?! OPEN THIS DOOR! NOW!!

*The door handle turns, the door swings wide, and massive amounts of
smoke suddenly billow through the back of the bus. The smoke clears to*

reveal Jay and Silent Bob squeezed into the bathroom, holding a massive joint.

JAY

Um . . . I think something's burning back here.

EXT. ROADSIDE—DAY

As the bus pulls away, Jay and Silent Bob are revealed, left behind.

JAY

The whole fucking world's against us, dude. I swear to God.

Silent Bob nods. Jay sticks out his thumb and starts hitching.

EXT. ROADSIDE—LATER

Jay and Bob are walking backwards, hitching still.

JAY

This sucks balls, man. How come we ain't getting no rides?

VOICE

'Cause you're doing it all wrong.

Jay and Bob look behind them. There's a GUY hitching as well.

GUY

You gotta induce the drivers a little.

JAY

Like how?

GUY

Like this.

The Guy holds out his sign to them. It reads: Will Give Head For Ride.

JAY

Yeah, but what happens when you get in the car, and you don't make with the head? Don't they kick your ass to the curb?

                                GUY
        Sure—if you don't make with the head.

Jay and Bob look at him for a long beat. Then . . .

                                JAY
        Eww! You eat the cock?!?

                                GUY
        Yeah. If it'll get me a few hundred miles across country, I'll take
        a shot in the mouth.

                                JAY
        Yeah, but we ain't gay.

                                GUY
        Well, neither am I. But have you seen the price of bus tickets
        lately? Shit—I don't wanna cough up two hundred bucks just to
        get to Chicago.

                                JAY
        Well, I don't wanna cough up some dude's sperm!

                                GUY
        Don't be so suburban—this is the new millenium. Gay,
        straight—it's all the same now. There're no more lines.

Jay draws a line on the ground with his foot.

                                JAY
        There's one. On this side of it, we ain't gay.

                                GUY
        All hitchers do this. Why do you think people pick us up? If you
        get a ride, it's expected—I don't care who the driver is. It's the
        first rule in the Book.

                                JAY
        What book?

                                GUY
        The unwritten Book of the Road.

A TRUCK *starts to pull over to the side of the road. The Guy points to it, as if to say "See?" The passenger-side door opens. The Guy climbs into the truck and closes the door. He looks out the window at Jay and Bob.*

> GUY
>
> Follow the rules of the Book, and you'll get where you're going in no time. Excuse me.

Through the windshield, Jay and Silent Bob see the Guy go face-first into the TRUCK DRIVER'S *lap. The Truck Driver smiles, and the truck takes off, roaring down the road.*

Jay and Silent Bob watch the truck disappear. Then, a CAR *pulls up. The* NUN *driving rolls down the passenger side window and leans toward them.*

> NUN
>
> You two boys need a ride?

INT. CAR—LATER

The Nun drives, smiling. Jay and Silent Bob sit in the back seat, huddled close together, their eyes glued on the Nun.

> NUN
>
> You both don't have to sit back there. One of you can sit up here with me.

Silent Bob shakes his head "no" to Jay. Jay shrugs and climbs up front.

> NUN
>
> So where are you boys from?

> JAY
>
> New Jersey.

> NUN
>
> What brings you to Indiana?

> JAY
>
> We're going to Hollywood.

> NUN
>
> Hollywood, hunh? That's a long ways away.

JAY

Yeah—we're lucky you picked us up.

NUN

Well, do unto others. That's what the Book says.

JAY

(misinterpreting completely)

Wait a minute—you follow the Book, too?

NUN

I live my life by it.

JAY

Really? *You?*

NUN

Of course. You know how lonely it gets on the road? Thanks to the Book, I'm never alone—if you know what I mean.

JAY

I guess. This guy back there explained it to us. But I didn't think *you'd* be into that.

NUN

Are you kidding? I've dedicated my life to it. Every hour of every day.

JAY

Shit—you nuns are alright.

NUN

You live by the Book, too?

JAY

You picked us up, didn't you? I gotta.

NUN

That's good to hear. But it takes deeds, not words. It's a lot easier to *say* you live by the Book than to actually *do* it.

(looks at him)

Can you do it?

JAY

You want me to do it right now?

NUN

No time like the present, right?

Jay looks back at Silent Bob. Silent Bob shakes his head "no." Jay shrugs, then flips his hair over his shoulder, and starts to bend down.

JAY

Alright.
                    (he suddenly stops)
Wait a sec—you a *Catholic* nun?

NUN

No. Presbyterian.

JAY
                    (looking at camera)
You hear that? She's not a Catholic. She's Presbyterian.

Jay disappears below the dash. The Nun goes wide-eyed.

EXT. ROADSIDE—DAY

The Nun's car screeches to the side of the road. Jay gets kicked out of the front seat by the screaming Nun. Silent Bob rushes out too, and the car races off. Jay's wipes his mouth. He pulls a long, curly hair from between his teeth.

JAY

Dude—she had seventies bush.

EXT. HIGHWAY—NIGHT

Jay and Bob continue hitching.

JAY

I can't believe this shit. Five hours and not a single ride. Every day, millions of people hitch to Hollywood and stop studios from making movies about 'em. But when you and me try it, it's like we're trapped in a fucking cartoon!

A familiar-looking VAN *pulls up on the other side of the road. The horn beeps. Jay and Bob look at each other, shrug, and race across the street, get in. The van pulls off.*

INT. VAN—NIGHT

Jay and Bob sit in the back of the van and stare at . . .

A clean-cut GUY, *a* BOOKISH *woman in glasses, a red-headed* BEAUTY, *a stoner* DUDE, *and a* GREAT DANE.

Jay looks at Silent Bob.

JAY

Zoinks, yo.

GUY

And now we can finally solve the mystery of the Hitchhiking Ghouls! Pull off their masks and let's see who they really are!

BOOKISH

I don't think they *are* masks.

BEAUTY

And I don't think they're Hitchhiking Girls either.

BOOKISH

Ghouls, you fucking moron. Not *Girls.*
(to herself)
Though I *wish* they were hitchhiking girls. Sexy, skimpily clad hitchhiking girls . . .

GUY

Let's kick them out. We've got a mystery to solve.

DUDE

The only mystery here is why we take our cues from a dick in a neckerchief!

GUY

Keep it up, Beatnik! I'll feed you to the fucking dog!

BEAUTY
(covering her ears; shrieking)
I CAN'T TAKE ALL THIS FIGHTING!

JAY

YO!

The Gang look to Jay and Bob.

JAY

Youse guys need to turn those frowns upside down! And we got
just the thing for that.
(pulls out a bag of joints)
We call them Doobie Snax.

INT. VAN—WEED-VISION

As Jay and Bob toke up, we go all SLO-MO *and '70s freaky (with the
image seeming to* SWIM*). Through their stoned haze, we see old-school
witches, skeletons, and ghouls swirling about their heads—the latter of
which gets his mask taken off to reveal a man inside a costume.*

*Jay and Bob look at the gang, then take a hit off their joint and look back.
Suddenly, the gang's engaged in total debauchery: the Dude rides the
windshield while the Guy cackles insanely, blindfolded by his neckerchief.
Bookish and Beauty are in their underwear, making out with each other.
The Great Dane looks at Jay and Bob and says . . .*

GREAT DANE
Ri, Ray rand Rirent Rob.

The Great Dane rolls over, revealing its RED THING *sticking way out of
its sheath. It's monstrous. Jay and Bob go wide-eyed.*

JAY
Look at his fuckin' lipstick!!! He's got a stoner-boner!!!

Jay and Bob smile and pass out.

*We cut back to the gang, who now appear as they did prior to Weed-
Vision. They stare at the O.C. Jay and Bob.*

BEAUTY
I think they passed out.

GUY
Great. What do we do with them now?

DUDE
Let's cut out their kidneys to sell on the black market and leave them in a seedy motel bathtub full of ice.

BOOKISH
Oh God, not again?

INT. SEEDY MOTEL BATHROOM—NIGHT

Jay lies in a bathtub full of ice, screaming. There's a scar on his back.

EXT. KANSAS CITY PARK—DAY

Jay wakes up suddenly, screaming. He startles Bob awake as well, as he clutches at his back, lifting his shirt to see the scar. It's not there.

JAY
Holy shit, I had a horrible dream.
(looks around)
Yo, I'm hungry. Where can we get some breakfast?

Bob looks around, and then locks on something O.C. He points, and Jay looks, smiles widely, and nods.

EXT. MOOBY'S FAST FOOD JOINT—DAY

An ESTABLISHING SHOT *of the fast food eatery, as Jay and Bob enter.*

INT. MOOBY'S FAST FOOD JOINT—SAME

As the pair head for the counter, Jay notices a public INTERNET TERMINAL. *He tugs at Silent Bob's arm.*

JAY
Yo—check that shit out: the Internet. Let's see if those fucks said something new about us and that stupid flick.

Bob shrugs, heading for the terminal. He inserts a dollar and types, following it up with a mouse click. The pair look at the screen and go wide-eyed.

JAY
(reading)
"Any movie based on Jay and Silent Bob is gonna lick balls,
because they both, in fact, lick balls. Namely each other's."

Jay and Silent Bob look at each other, wide-eyed.

JAY

Eww.
(reading further)
"Yes—they are real people. Real *stupid* people. Signed, Darth
Randal."
(to Bob)
Motherfucker! It's time *we* wrote something *back!* Type this shit
down.

Silent Bob starts typing as Jay dictates.

JAY

All you motherfuckers are gonna pay. You are the ones who are
the ball-lickers. We're gonna fuck your mothers while you watch
and cry like little bitches. Once we get to Hollywood and find
those Miramax fucks who are making the movie, we're gonna
make 'em eat our shit, then shit out our shit, then eat *their* shit
which is made up of our shit that we made 'em eat. Then all you
motherfuckers are next. Love, Jay and Silent Bob.

*Silent Bob finishes typing and presses 'Return'. He and Jay nod at each
other, then head over to the counter line, looking up at the menu board.*

JAY

That'll fucking show 'em. Now we eat our Egga-Mooby-Muffins,
then get back on the road, get to Hollywood, and stop that fucking
movie from getting made. No more hairy-bush nuns, no more
dogs. We keep our eye on the prize, and not let nothing—and I
mean NOTHING—distract us.

As Jay finishes speaking, he looks to the O.C. doors and freezes.

*A gorgeous GIRL walks through the front doors, all in SLO-MO, to the
tune of Prince's The Most Beautiful Girl in the World. She's bathed in
light, glowing. She bats her eyelashes, gliding toward us.*

Jay is mouth-agape wide-eyed. Silent Bob looks at him, then at the O.C. Girl. He slowly waves his hand in front of Jay's eyes, getting zero response.

JAY'S POV: The Girl smiles at us. His POV goes from her face, down to her breasts, then down to her crotch.

Jay moves past Silent Bob and meets the Girl in the middle of the floor. He embraces her and lands a long, sweet kiss on her mouth. After a beat, he starts fumbling like a teenager to get to second base under her shirt, totally incongruous with the music. The Girl kindly tries to deter him.

But it's just a fantasy. Jay's still standing there next to Silent Bob, but he is sporting a huge BONER. Silent Bob rolls his eyes. He grabs a soda cup off the counter and sticks it over Jay's boner, just as the Girl joins them in line. She smiles at the zombified Jay.

> GIRL
> *(off cup)*
> Oh my God. Do you get free refills with that?

> JAY
> Oh, what—this? I just wear this for protection. You know—so no guys try to grab my shit.

> GIRL
> I never thought of that. I'm gonna have to steal your idea.

> JAY
> Go ahead—you already stole my heart.

The Girl chuckles and extends her hand to Jay and Bob.

> GIRL
> Hi. I'm Justice.

> JAY
> *(dreamily)*
> And I am so fucking yours . . .

Silent Bob pokes Jay, who shakes off his daze.

> JAY
> I mean hi. I'm Jay, and this is my hetero life-mate, Silent Bob.

JUSTICE

It's nice to meet you.

JAY

Justice, hunh? That's a nice name.
(under his breath, to Bob)
Jay 'n' Justice, sitting in a tree. F-U-C-K-I-N-G . . .
(back to Justice)
So you come here often?

JUSTICE

Oh, I'm not from around here. My friends and I are taking a road
trip, and we just stopped to grab something to eat.

JAY

Your friends, hunh? Where they at?

JUSTICE

(pointing)
Out there. By that van.

Jay and Bob look past Justice to see a VAN with three other gorgeous
GIRLS stretching outside of it, throwing their hair around, looking
incredibly sexy. Without looking at Silent Bob, Jay quietly says to him . . .

JAY

Dude—I think I just filled the cup.

INT. VAN—DAY

Jay and Bob climb into the van, getting odd looks from the other Girls.
Justice follows them in, tossing the fast food to her friends.

JAY

Ladies, ladies, ladies! Jay and Silent Bob are in the hizz-ouse!!!

SISSY

Who the fuck are these guys?

JUSTICE

This is Jay and Silent Bob.
(to Jay and Bob)
Guys, this is Sissy, Missy, and Chrissy.

CHRISSY
Where the fuck did they come from?

JUSTICE
I met 'em inside. They're gonna hitch a ride.

SISSY
I don't know if that's such a great idea, Jussy.

JAY
Sure it is, Juggs.

MISSY
Oh my God—he just called Sissy "Juggs"!

CHRISSY
I'm on it.

Chrissy lunges toward Jay, pulling a knife.

JUSTICE
Chrissy, no!

Sissy stops Chrissy, shoving a burger into her hands.

SISSY
We're in the middle of suburbia, *Chrissy*. Let's try to act like it.

CHRISSY
And what—stupid-ass little foul-mouthed bitch-boys *don't* get
their balls cut off in suburbia?

JAY
(*oblivious*)
What's with the knife? We having cake or something?

CHRISSY
Holy shit—he's retarded, to boot.

JAY
(*to Silent Bob*)
Yo—she called you retarded.

SISSY
(to Justice)
What's wrong with you, Justice? You *do* remember where we're
going, don't you?

MISSY
That we have a *job* to do?

JUSTICE
They're just gonna tag along for a few miles. They won't get in
the way. I promise.
(cutesy)
Please?

SISSY
I swear, I don't know what's going on in that head of yours lately.

Sissy looks at her for a long beat, then relents.

SISSY
Fine—they can ride with us. But they're so out of here before we
get to Boulder.

JUSTICE
Honest Injun.

CHRISSY
"Honest Injun"?
(to Sissy)
I can't believe what a pushover you are.

JAY
And I can't believe fine-ass bitches like yourselves eat *that* shit.
Don't you know fast food makes girls fart?

Suddenly, Jay and Bob are parted by BRENT, *who's getting into the van.*

BRENT
Say—what's all this talk about farting?

*Sissy, Missy, and Chrissy immediately go from disgusted to sweet and airy,
totally switching characters.*

SISSY/CHRISSY/MISSY

Hi, Brent!

SISSY

This is Brent. He's with us, too.

CHRISSY

Brent, tell these sillies that girls don't fart.

BRENT

Of course they don't! Only skeevy stoners fart.

The very white Brent puts his hand out to be slapped by Jay and Silent Bob.

BRENT

What up, homies?
(off the Girls)
Wow. Three guys, four girls . . .
(to Jay and Bob)
What's the count, boys?

Jay and Bob look at each other and roll their eyes.

EXT. HIGHWAY—DAY

The van drives down the road. We hear singing from inside.

INT. VAN—DAY

Brent strums a guitar and sings, as the Girls and Jay and Bob listen, rolling eyes.

BRENT

Hey there mister science-guy
don't spray that aeresol in my eye
for I don't really want to die
I'm a noble rabbit!

JAY

What're you guys, like a cover band or something?

SISSY

We're the Kansas State chapter of S.A.A.C.—Students Against
Animal Cruelty.

CHRISSY

And we're on our way to Colorado to give Provasik a piece of our
minds!

Everyone lets out a whoop, except Jay and Bob.

JAY

What the fuck are you bitches babbling about?

BRENT

Hey! Watch the language, little boy. There are females present.

Jay and Silent Bob eyeball Brent, until Justice distracts them.

JUSTICE

Provasik Pharmaceuticals is a medical lab where they peform
gross experiments on animals.

JAY

So, what kind of animals are we talking about here—like bears
and rhinos?

BRENT

No—more like rabbits, dogs, cats . . . heck, even monkeys. If we
don't speak for them, who will?
   (touches Justice's arm)
Right, Jussy?

*Jay sees this and his eyes flare over the competition. After a beat, he
relaxes.*

JAY

Hey, uh—Brent? Can I talk to you over here for a second?

Brent joins Jay, strumming his guitar. Jay addresses him confidentially.

JAY

Be honest, yo—you're down with this for the fine-ass pussy,
right?

                    BRENT
I'm down with this because I love animals, stupid.

                    JAY
Even sheep?

                    BRENT
Of course. Sheep are beautiful creatures.

                    JAY
They are beautiful, aren't they?

                    BRENT
Oh God, yes.

                    JAY
So then you'd fuck a sheep?

                    BRENT
What is your damage, little boy? You've got a sick and twisted
world perspective.

                    JAY
No, you misunderstand me, Prince Valiant. I mean if you were
another sheep. Would you fuck a sheep if you were another
sheep?

                    BRENT
I . . . suppose so.

                    JAY
That's what I thought.
                (suddenly loudly, to all)
YO! THIS MOTHERFUCKER AIN'T ONE OF US! HE JUST
SAID HE'D FUCK A SHEEP!

EXT. HIGHWAY—DAY

*The side door of the van slides open and Brent gets hurled out of the
moving vehicle. Jay throws his guitar at him as well, yelling and flipping
the bird as the van drives off.*

                    JAY
YA DIRTY SHEEP FUCKER!!!

EXT. HIGHWAY—LATER

The van drives down the road.

INT. VAN—SAME

Missy drives. Sissy sits in the passenger seat. Chrissy kneels between them.

> CHRISSY
>
> What the fuck are we gonna do now?

> SISSY
>
> Shut up, I'm thinking.

In the back, Justice studies some blueprints. Jay joins her, and she quickly folds them up.

> JAY
>
> Is Hollywood near where we're going?

> JUSTICE
>
> Is that where you guys are from?

> JAY
>
> Ch'yeah, right. Jersey represent!

> JUSTICE
>
> Oh, a Jersey Boy. What brings you all the way out here?

> JAY
>
> Well, we couldn't hang in front of the Quick Stop no more, 'cause of the strainen-en order, which sucks ass 'cause it's been like our home since we were kids. Silent Bob even busted his cherry there.

> JUSTICE
> *(to Bob)*
>
> You did? I'll bet she was a lucky girl.

Bob blushes. Jay doesn't like that Justice's attention has strayed.

> JAY
>
> Look, fuck that fat fuck—I'm trying to tell a story here.

JUSTICE

Sorry.

JAY

Anyway, we were talking to Brodie and he said there's gonna be a Bluntman and Chronic movie. So we went to see Holden McNeil, and he showed us the Internet, and that's where we found all these fucking little jerkoffs were saying shit about us. So we decided to go to Hollywood and stop the movie from getting made. And now we're here.

JUSTICE

Wow. I have *no idea* what you just said.

JAY

Yeah, I get that a lot. So you like animals, hunh?

JUSTICE

Sure.

JAY

That's cool. Even snakes?

JUSTICE

You can't exclude an animal just because it's not cuddly. Of course I like snakes.

JAY

How about *trouser* snakes?

JUSTICE

What's a trouser snake?

Just then, a little JAY DEVIL appears on Jay's left shoulder.

JAY DEVIL
(to Jay)
What the fuck are you waiting for? She went for the setup! Reach in your fucking pants, and pull yer cock out, bitch! That's the kinda shit girls like!

Suddenly, another little JAY DEVIL appears on Jay's right shoulder.

JAY DEVIL 2

Right about here's where the angel's supposed to show up and
tell you *not* to pull your dick out. But we bitch-slapped that little
fuck and sent him packing, so it's smooth sailing. Let 'er rip, boy!

*They disappear in little puffs of smoke and Jay shoves his hand down his
pants, getting ready to whip out his dick, when suddenly, a little JAY
ANGEL appears on his shoulder, rubbing a swollen jaw.*

JAY ANGEL

Sorry I'm late. So what's the deal here?
(looks down)
Oh, shit—you're not thinking of whipping your dick out at this
fine piece of woman, are you?

Jay thinks, then nods "Yes." The Jay Angel rolls his eyes, and slaps him.

JAY ANGEL

Tell you what: look at Silent Bob. See if *he* thinks it's a good idea
to whip your dick out.

*Jay looks to Silent Bob. Silent Bob looks from Jay's hand in his pants to
Jay and shakes his head "No," sternly. Jay withdraws his hand from his
pants. The Jay Angel nods, satisfied.*

JAY ANGEL

That's it, boy—put the dick down. You gotta go from the heart,
yo. No little perv bullshit will do for *this* one. Be smooth. Be Don
Juan de la Nootch. Now I gotta go beat the shit out of two sucker-
punching little bitches. Remember—don't pull your dick out until
she asks you to.
(beat)
Or until she's sleeping. Bunnnnggg!

The Jay Angel blinks away. Justice looks at Jay, a bit confused.

JAY

Don't ask.
(beat)
So, uh . . . what can a pimp-daddy like me do to help the animals?

JUSTICE

You really don't want to help us . . .

JAY

What the fuck are you talking about? Sure, I do. I'd do *anything* for you.

Justice smiles. Jay tries to recover.

JAY

I mean, youse *guys!* I'd do anything for *youse* guys. For the lift and shit.

JUSTICE

You sure?

JAY

Sure, I'm sure. I said it, didn't I? Fuck.

JUSTICE

Well . . . okay. Let me talk it over with the other girls and get back to you.

JAY

You do that.

Jay takes Justice's hand and kisses it.

JAY

I'll be right here.

He winks at her, smiles, and moves to the other side of the van, near Silent Bob. He's still smiling at Justice and winking when he looks to Silent Bob, who stares at him blankly, then imitates Jay's hand-kissing back at him. Jay scowls.

JAY

Fuck you, Fatty.

EXT. CONVENIENCE STORE—DAY

The van pulls up and all pile out, stretching. The Girls head toward the store. Justice calls over to Jay and Silent Bob.

JUSTICE

You guys want anything from inside?

JAY

No, we're cool, thanks, hon.

Justice smiles and heads inside. Jay and Silent Bob study the front of the foreign convenience store. They look for a place to lean, try a few spots out, then settle into one. After a beat . . .

JAY

It just ain't the same, is it? This place licks balls compared to Quick Stop.

Silent Bob shakes his head "Yeah."

JAY

And speaking of licking balls—how 'bout that Justice chick? She is too fine. And she smells so fucking pretty. She's got a nice voice, too. And that body? Smoking. You know, she never *once* said "fuck off," when I was talking to her, or pulled out pepper spray, or nothing. I tell ya, Lunchbox—she could be the one.

INT. CONVENIENCE STORE—DAY

Justice is at the microwave when she's suddenly surrounded by the other Girls.

MISSY

Smooth move, Justice.

CHRISSY
(slapping Justice upside the head)
Nice going, Four Eyes!

JUSTICE

Ow!

SISSY

Why the fuck did you let that little stoner throw Brent out of the van?!

JUSTICE

Oh, please—if I had to listen to one more of those stupid songs, I was going to throw him out *myself.*

SISSY

We needed Brent, Justice! He was our *patsy!*

JUSTICE

We'll just find someone else. Besides, I didn't see you trying to stop Jay from throwing him out.

SISSY

Because I didn't want to blow our cover!

JUSTICE

Cover, shmover—you all hated his songs, too.

CHRISSY

Not as much as I hate you.

Justice offers Chrissy a cold glance.

CHRISSY

Fuck, if I don't get to kill someone soon, I'm gonna . . . fucking *kill* someone!

SISSY
(rubbing Chrissy's shoulders)
Don't mind Chrissy. She's just a little too wound for sound.

CHRISSY

Then how about you help me take the edge off?

Chrissy grabs Missy forcefully and the pair make out, hot and heavy in the middle of the convenience store. Other customers regard them wide-eyed.

JUSTICE
(to Customers)
They're *really* good friends.

SISSY
(to Chrissy and Missy)
Would you two knock it off? We're in the fucking heartland here! Try to blend.

JUSTICE

They already do—she's the milkmaid, and she's the cow.

CHRISSY

Oh, I'm a cow, am I? I'm a mad cow, bitch. And now I'm gonna rip your head off and fuck your spine stump.

SISSY

Enough!
(calm, to Justice)
We have a very simple gang here, Justice. I'm the brains, Chrissy's the brawn, and Missy's the tech-girl. But lately, I'm having a hard time figuring out what *you're* doing here.

JUSTICE

That makes two of us.

CHRISSY

Shit—your *name* doesn't even fit the rhyme scheme.

JUSTICE

That's because very few names rhyme with "douchebag."

CHRISSY
(getting in her face)
You're dancing on my last nerve, Strawberry Shortcake.
(to Sissy)
You deal with the weak link. I'm gonna take Missy into the dirty convenience store bathroom and hate-fuck the shit out of her.

Chrissy drags Missy off. Justice and Sissy watch them go.

JUSTICE

And you said letting them read all that Anaïs Nin wouldn't amount to anything.

SISSY

Don't change the subject. You *know* what you have to do now, right? Since you let our patsy slip away, you've gotta convince the little kid and the fat guy to take his place. *They've* gotta break into Provasik now.

JUSTICE

Uh-uh!

SISSY

Uh-*huh.* You'll do it, or you're out of this gang. Just use the little one's crush to convince him, since he's so fucking in love with you.

JUSTICE

Jay? No he's not.

SISSY

What—am I blind? He *wasn't* kissing your hand back in the van like he was fucking Lord Byron?

JUSTICE

Well, maybe he was just raised with manners.

EXT. CONVENIENCE STORE—DAY

A GIRL *walks past Jay and Bob, heading out of the store.*

JAY
(to exited Girl)
YO, BABY! YOU EVER HAVE YOUR ASSHOLE LICKED BY A FAT MAN IN AN OVERCOAT?!
(to Bob)
Yeah.

INT. CONVENIENCE STORE—DAY

Sissy continues to confront Justice.

SISSY

You're the one that brought the kid in, Jussy. So *you've* gotta make amends.

JUSTICE

Jay is *not* taking Brent's place as the patsy.

SISSY

That kid and his quiet friend are our only options at this point. Now, we got about two hours before we get to Boulder. That gives you plenty of time to work on him.

JUSTICE

I'm not gonna do it.

SISSY

Why the fuck not?

JUSTICE

Because he's just so innocent!

Justice looks out the window and smiles, seeing Jay dancing alongside Bob.

JUSTICE

Look at him . . .

EXT. CONVENIENCE STORE—SAME

Jay's dancing still, but now we hear what he's SINGING to Silent Bob.

JAY

I'm gonna finger-fuck her tight little asshole! Finger-bang . . . and tea-bag my balls . . . in her mouth! Where? Where? In her mouth . . . balls-a-plenty in her mouth! Balls, balls, sweaty balls . . .

INT. CONVENIENCE STORE—SAME

Sissy eyeballs Justice, who's still looking out at Jay.

SISSY

Who's it going to be, Jussy—him or us?

Justice looks at Sissy. Sissy nods at her. Justice looks back out at Jay.

INT. VAN—DAY

Justice talks to Jay and Silent Bob.

JAY

Steal a monkey? Shit—no problem.

JUSTICE

It's not really *stealing*—it's *liberating* it, and . . .
(*finally hears him*)
Wait a second—did you say, "No problem"?

JAY

Yeah. Fuck—we steal monkeys all the time.

                    (to Bob)

Right, Lunchbox?

Silent Bob glares at Jay.

JUSTICE

It's not like it's a bad thing. It's for a good cause.

JAY

Oh, it's for the best cause, *mon cheri* . . .

                    (takes her hand)

The cause of love.

                    (kisses her hand, then releases)

Snoogans . . .

JUSTICE

What the heck is that?

JAY

What's what?

JUSTICE

"Snoogans," I believe it was.

JAY

What the fuck do you think it means? It means "I'm kidding."

JUSTICE

Ohhh. Well, that's too bad.

She smiles at Jay, touches his chin, and heads to the front of the van. Jay plays it cool until she's out of sight, then humps Silent Bob's leg like a dog.

JAY

                    (singing)

I can't believe I'm gonna get some pussy for stealing a monkey!

                    (speaking)

If I'd known it was that easy, I'd've been stealing monkeys since I was like seven and shit.

Jay looks at Silent Bob, who clearly disapproves.

                              JAY
Don't, motherfucker. Don't you ruin this for me. Me and Justice
are gonna get married one day, so don't be giving me that "we-
ain't-stealing-no-monkey" look. I'm Morris Day; you're Jerome,
bitch. Don't forget that. That girl? That girl's in love with me.

Up front, Justice talks to Sissy, while Missy drives.

                            JUSTICE
They're gonna do it.

                             SISSY
Good. They do their part . . .
                    (pats a video camera)
And we'll do ours.

Justice eyes Sissy, then slumps in her seat.

EXT. PROVASIK MEDICAL LABS—NIGHT

*The van rolls up across the street from the Provasik Labs, parking in front
of another large building.*

INT. VAN—SAME

*Jay and Silent Bob get out, along with Justice. They wear Ninja masks.
Missy and Chrissy follow.*

                            JUSTICE
Remember—we meet back here when you're done. You sure
you're okay with this?

                              JAY
As sure as I am that you're the hottest bitch I ever seen.

Chrissy lunges at Jay. Missy holds her back, dragging Chrissy away.

                              JAY
What's twisting that bitch's tits?

                            JUSTICE
Maybe it's because women don't like to be called "bitches," Jay.

JAY

They don't? Well how 'bout "piece of ass"?

JUSTICE

How about not.

JAY

Well, what the fuck am I supposed to call you, then?

JUSTICE

Something sweet, you big goof. Something nice.

JAY
(thinks; then)

Boo-Boo Kitty Fuck.

JUSTICE
(laughing)

Okay. That's a start.

Sissy jumps out of the van, holding the video camera, aiming it at Jay and Bob.

SISSY

Jay, before you go, could you say something into the camera about the clitoris.

JAY

What?

JUSTICE
(to Sissy)

Man, you are such a bitch . . .

SISSY
(off Justice; to Jay)

She's just a little embarrassed. See, Jussy and I are putting together this documentary for our Human Sexuality class, and we need a male perspective on the clitoris.

JAY

The *female* clitoris?

SISSY

Uh . . . yeah.

JUSTICE

Jay, you don't have to do this.

She elbows Sissy.

JAY

Nah, it's cool, hon. There's a few things I can say about the clit
that I'd like you to hear.
                (clears throat; into camera)
I am the *master* of the clit! I make that shit *work!* It does whatever
the *fuck* I tell it to do! No one rules the clit like *me!*
                (off Silent Bob)
Not *this* little fuck! None of you little fucks out there! I am the
clit *commander!!!* Remember that—commander of all clits!

*Jay proceeds to make some pussy-eating faces. Justice shakes her head at
Sissy, who snaps the camera closed and smiles.*

SISSY

Awesome. Knock 'em dead, Tiger.

Sissy climbs back into the van.

JAY
(to Justice)
So . . . can I get a little kiss for good luck?

Justice smiles at Jay, then kisses him sweetly on the lips.

JAY

So . . . can I get a little blow job for good luck?

*Justice smiles and pulls Jay's mask down. He heads off, revealing Silent
Bob behind him, lips puckered, hanging in midair. Jay reaches back into
the frame, pulling Bob out. Justice watches them go.*

SISSY

Jussy. C'mon.

Justice climbs back into the van.

INT. VAN—SAME

Justice sits, glaring at Sissy.

> SISSY
>
> Hey. Lover-girl. You cock-block my authority again, you lose your fucking fronts, you got that?

> JUSTICE
>
> Yes, sir.

Sissy takes the tape out of the camera and hands it off to Missy, beside whom is a bag full of high-tech equipment.

> SISSY
>
> Phase One, down. While we're executing Phase Two, you edit that tape and grab a new car.

> MISSY
>
> No sweat.

> SISSY
>
> Let's suit up.

EXT. PROVASIK MEDICAL LABS—NIGHT

Jay and Silent Bob tuck-and-roll across the front lawn, stopping at the building. Silent Bob pulls a GRAPPLING GUN out of his coat. He fires it into the air as Jay quickly gives the "metal" sign, and the pair are lifted out-of-frame.

INT. PROVASIK MEDICAL LABS—NIGHT

It's dead quiet and still. Then, the pair smash through a window, landing on the floor in a ball. They lift their Ninja hoods. Jay glares at Silent Bob.

> JAY
>
> You fat fuck . . .

INT. VAN—NIGHT

Missy peers through binoculars out the window.

                              SISSY
      They in?

                              MISSY
      You can say that.

                              SISSY
      Time to shine. Let's go.

EXT. VAN—NIGHT

*The quartet piles out of the van, and we get our first good look at them:
sexily geared up for action, wearing all black. They head for a
SEPARATE BUILDING, stopping at the front door.*

*Sissy gestures elaborately to Missy, and Missy gestures elaborately back,
racing away into the night. Justice offers Sissy a look.*

                              JUSTICE
      You are *so* gay.

*Chrissy sticks a box on the door and presses a button. On a digital
readout, numbers roll until they stop on four different digits. The door
lock CLICKS open.*

                              SISSY
      Once we're inside, I want complete silence.
                    (holding up high-tech device)
      Missy whipped this up. It counts our decibel level. If it goes into
      the red—alarm, we're dead. So not even the slightest noise, got
      it?

*Justice blows her off. Sissy enters the building, followed closely by
Chrissy. Justice lingers at the door, taking one last look back at the
Provasik Building, fretting for Jay and Bob.*

                              SISSY
                    (pokes her head back out)
      Justice! Move your ass!

Justice heads inside. We PAN up to reveal a sign that reads: BOULDER
DIAMOND EXCHANGE.

INT. PROVASIK TESTING ROOM—NIGHT

Jay and Bob stand there, looking around the room.

It's lined with cages, all of which contain sad-looking ANIMALS.

A tear forms in Silent Bob's eye. Jay rolls his eyes and hits him.

JAY
Stay frosty, you big fucking softie. We've got a job to do.

Silent Bob nods and clicks on a flashlight. The pair wade through the cages. Jay stops at an EMERGENCY BOX hanging on the wall. Inside it, there's a pistol.

JAY
Check this out, Lunchbox. Animal tranquilizer! This shit *fucks* you up like Percocets!

Jay elbows the glass, breaking it. He takes the gun out and tosses it to Bob.

JAY
Hold this. Later, me and Justice can shoot each other with it and fuck like stoned test bunnies. Bunnggg.

Silent Bob rolls his eyes and sticks the gun in his coat. The pair look through the cages, until they HEAR the distinct SOUND OF A MONKEY. Jay directs Silent Bob's flashlight to the cage from where the sound emitted. He smiles.

JAY
(reading)
"Suzanne." Boo-yah.

INT. BOULDER DIAMOND EXCHANGE—NIGHT

The three Girls stand at the end of a large hallway. At the other end is a glass case, full of DIAMONDS.

Sissy pulls an aerosol can from her utility belt and sprays the air in the hallway. She watches the decibel monitor, which rises only slightly at the sound of the spray. Suddenly, within the mist, laser beams become apparent.

Sissy hands the decibel monitor to Chrissy and takes a few steps back, shaking her hands to limber up. She then runs forward and does an impressive series of flips down the hallway, not touching a single laser beam.

Chrissy checks the decibel monitor, which rises only slightly.

Once Sissy's flipping comes to a stop at the other end of the hallway near the Diamond case, she makes a hand gesture to Justice. Justice nods, and proceeds to do the same series of flips down the hallway, not tripping the alarm.

Chrissy checks the decibel monitor, which rises only slightly.

Justice lands beside Sissy, and then Sissy gestures to Chrissy.

Chrissy tosses the decibel monitor over the laser beams. Sissy catches it, and the monitor rises only slightly.

Then, Chrissy proceeds with her series of flips, which are even more impressive than the other two, including running up walls and pushing off into handstand flips. When she passes the last laser beam, she lands between Sissy and Justice, arms in the air like a gymnast. Then, she lets out a loud, manly FART.

The decibel monitor goes red and an alarm starts RINGING through the building.

CHRISSY

Holy fuck—the little stoner was right . . .

Sissy shatters the glass surrounding the Diamonds. She pours them into a bag, and races back down the hallway, followed by Justice and Chrissy.

EXT. BOULDER DIAMOND EXCHANGE—NIGHT

The Girls emerge from the Diamond Exchange, just as Missy pulls up in a CONVERTIBLE.

CHRISSY

Boom box!

Missy tosses a metal box to Chrissy, who catches it and races toward the van, while Sissy and Justice pile into the convertible.

> SISSY
>
> I can't believe it. Months of planning and it's all blown by a fucking fart . . .

> JUSTICE
>
> We can't just leave them like this! That alarm's gonna bring the cops here any minute!

> SISSY
>
> That was always the plan, Justice! They take the heat off us long enough until we can get out of town!

Chrissy attaches the metal box to the side of the van.

> CHRISSY
>
> Kaboom, you little stoner fucks.

The girls pull up in the convertible and Chrissy jumps into the car with them.

> CHRISSY
>
> It's set. Let's roll.

The convertible screeches away, leaving the van sitting there. The metal box magnetically attached to the side is counting down from two minutes.

INT. PROVASIK TESTING LAB—NIGHT

Jay and Bob carry a large canvas bag between them. Something seems to move inside it. They head for the exit, but Silent Bob hesitates, offering a sad look to the animals in all the cages. Jay hits him.

> JAY
>
> What the fuck are you looking at? There ain't no snacks here, man! Now we got what we came for, so let's get the fuck out!

Silent Bob half-gestures to the cages, forlorn. Jay shakes his head, frustrated.

> JAY
>
> Yeah, it's sad! But what the fuck are *we* supposed to do about it?

Silent Bob offers Jay a look.

EXT. PROVASIK MEDICAL LABS—NIGHT

The front doors burst open, spilling out Jay, Silent Bob (carrying their bag), and HUNDREDS OF ANIMALS—*cats, dogs, birds, rabbits. All race off into the night.*

Jay and Bob race toward the van. Jay screams at it.

> JAY
> JUSTICE! OPEN THE DOORS!

Suddenly, Jay and Bob stop dead in their tracks.

> JAY
>
> Oh shit . . .

Three COP CARS *screech up, the van between them and Jay and Bob. The* COPS *leap out of their cruisers, guns drawn. Jay looks to Bob, pissed.*

> COP
> DROP THE BAG! NOW! BEFORE THIS THING TURNS EXPLOSIVE!

The counter on the device attached to the van hits "0," and the van BLOWS UP. *Jay and Bob get thrown backwards in one direction, the Cops in the other.*

On all fours, Jay looks at the burning shell of the van, a tear forming in his eye.

> JAY
>
> Justice . . .

We crane up from him as he bellows . . .

> JAY
> JUUUUUUSSSSSTTTTIIIIIIIICCCCCCE!!!!!

Silent Bob grabs Jay and drags him out-of-frame, still carrying the bag.

EXT. FEDERAL WILDLIFE MARSHAL'S OFFICE—DAY

We start on a sign on the door that reads: **Federal Wildlife Marshal, Colorado Field Office,** *then pull back to see a* DEPUTY *opening the door and heading inside.*

INT. FEDERAL WILDLIFE MARSHAL'S OFFICE—DAY

The Deputy enters just as a FAX *is coming through at an operations board. He rips it off, reading it. His eyes go wide.*

> DEPUTY
> Oh, fudge . . .
> *(calling off)*
> Marshal Willenholly!

INT. BATHROOM—SAME

MARSHAL WILLENHOLLY *sits on the bowl, staring at* Four Legged Law-Man *magazine, eyeing it lustily. Below frame, he jerks off.*

> WILLENHOLLY
> Yeah, you chug that ass-cock, baby . . . It takes two hands to hold, doesn't it . . . ? Uhhh . . .

As he climaxes, a banging at the door disrupts him.

> WILLENHOLLY
> WHAT?! WHAT?! I'M READING!

> DEPUTY (O.C.)
> Sir, we got a report of a break-in at Provasik Pharmaceuticals' testing lab.

Willenholly emerges from the bathroom, holding the magazine. There's a massive wet spot on the front of his pants.

> WILLENHOLLY
> Have you read this article on the mule-suckers in Tijuana? Good God, I wish that was in our jurisdiction—I'd shut down every last one of those ass-cock chuggers, personally.

The Deputy looks at the stain on Willenholly's pants, then at Willenholly.

WILLENHOLLY
What? "Ass" means "donkey."

DEPUTY
Yes, sir.
(hands him a fax)
This came in for you.

WILLENHOLLY
(looks at fax)
Boulder, hunh? Well, gas up the jet.

DEPUTY
We don't have a jet, sir. And Boulder's only ten minutes away.

WILLENHOLLY
Then gas up the next best thing.

EXT. PROVASIK MEDICAL LABS—DAY

There are FIRE TRUCKS *all over the place now. The burned out van is being poured over by Cops. Just then, Willenholly pulls up on a* MOPED. *He parks it and surveys the wreckage.*

WILLENHOLLY
My, oh my, oh my. Who let the cats out?
(thinks)
Wait . . . is that right?

COP 1 (O.C.)
Excuse me—who the hell are you?

Willenholly rips down the Velcro patch on his jacket, revealing a badge.

WILLENHOLLY
Federal Wildlife Marshal. This investigation is now under my jurisdiction.

COP 1
Oh really? And why's that?

WILLENHOLLY
Because someone let a whole mess of animals out of their cages, sir.

COP 1

Well, we believe that was just a diversionary tactic used to call attention away from the real heist over here at the Diamond Exchange.

WILLENHOLLY

Yeah—right. *That's* a believable scenario. It sounds more like something out of a bad movie.

Willenholly and the Cop look at the camera. Then, another COP *joins them.*

COP 2

Sir, the Provasik people say they've rounded all their animals up, except for one: an orangutan.

WILLENHOLLY

The most dangerous animal known to man . . .

Willenholly spins around to face the ten or so COPS *milling about, calling out.*

WILLENHOLLY

Listen up, ladies and gentlemen! Our fugitive has been on the run for six hours! Average simian foot speed over uneven ground— barring injuries or preoccupation with tire tubes, mites or bananas—is four miles an hour. That gives us a radius of twenty miles.

COP 3
(calling out from crowd)

Twenty-four, sir!

WILLENHOLLY

What?

COP 3

Six hours times four miles an hour is twenty-four.

WILLENHOLLY
(doing the math in his head)

Yes. Yes, you're right. My bad. Twenty-*four* miles. Now what I want out of all of you is a hard target search . . .

                              COP 4
Excuse me, sir?

                          WILLENHOLLY
Yeah?

                              COP 4
What does that mean, exactly—a "hard target search"? What's a
"hard target"?

                          WILLENHOLLY
Well, it's . . . a target . . . that's . . . *hard.* Anyway . . .

                              COP 4
So are you referring to the *search's* level of difficulty? Or is the
hard target the *monkey?*

                              COP 3
Or the people who *stole* the monkey?

The COPS *now chatter amongst themselves, to the effect of "Yeah . . . It
could mean that too . . . He's got a point . . . ," etc. Willenholly rubs his
temples.*

                          WILLENHOLLY
Okay, how about this? What I want out of all of you is a *thorough*
search of every gas station, residence, warehouse, farmhouse,
henhouse, outhouse, and doghouse in that area! Checkpoints go
up at fifteen miles!

                              COP 1
Wouldn't it make more sense to put them up at every twenty-*four*
miles—seeing as that's how far they'd have gotten in the last six
hours?

*They begin chattering amongst themselves again. Willenholly looks at
them all, defeated. He starts to cry.*

                          WILLENHOLLY
This is so frustrating. It's just so hard sometimes . . .
                            (yelling)
YOUR FUGITIVE'S NAME IS *SUZANNE!* GO FIND HER!

Another COP *joins Willenholly, carrying a large, fat envelope.*

> COP 5
>
> Sir, this was just delivered to the station.

> WILLENHOLLY
>
> What is it?

> COP 5
>
> It's a tape from the terrorists who're claiming credit for the break-in.

> WILLENHOLLY
>
> Is it VHS or Beta? You know what—never mind. Do you have a VCR?

INT. OFFICE—DAY

Willenholly and the Cops stare at the O.C. TV, *shocked, as the video ends.*

> WILLENHOLLY
>
> Oh my God . . .
> *(without looking up)*
> Have the jet gassed-up and ready to go at a moment's notice.

> COP
>
> Sir, we don't have a jet; just a helicopter.

> WILLENHOLLY
> *(dialing his cell phone)*
> Doesn't *anybody* have a jet anymore?
> *(into cell phone)*
> Plafsky? It's Willenholly. You gotta get me on the national news, pronto. Why?! Because we may very well be dealing with the two most dangerous men on the planet!

EXT. UTAH ROADSIDE—DAY

Jay and Silent Bob sit close to each other, staring at . . .

SUZANNE *(the* ORANGUTAN*)—who sits on a log across from them, staring back.*

                              JAY
This is Jussy's monkey.
                    (to Suzanne, angrily)
JUSTICE DIED FOR YOU, YOU MONKEY FUCK!

Suzanne covers her eyes with her hands suddenly. Jay and Silent Bob startle, with Jay leaping behind Silent Bob and pulling back as if he's going to strike.

                              JAY
                        (to Silent Bob)
Do something, Tons of Fun!

Silent Bob offers the ape a weak wave. Suzanne drops her hands from her face and waves back. Jay cranes his neck to see over Silent Bob.

                              JAY
Is that fucking thing waving at us?

Suzanne nods. Jay steps out from behind Bob. They stare at the ape.

                              JAY
Holy shit! That monkey understood us! Maybe it's some sort of super-monkey!

Suzanne offers them a "raspberry," spitting as if the comment was ridiculous. Jay and Silent Bob react with surprise at this.

                              JAY
What the fuck was that for? It's not a stupid idea! I seen it in *Congo*!

Suzanne holds her nose, as if to say "Congo stunk." Silent Bob smiles in agreement and amusement. Jay looks at him, stung.

                              JAY
You're *my* bitch. You get *my* back. Don't go joining this chimp's side.

Jay looks around the woods, formulating a thought. Silent Bob moves toward the ape, extending his hand to shake hers.

                                    JAY
        Yo—what if there's more super-monkeys up at that lab? Maybe
        they're making an army of 'em up there! Holy shit! Maybe it's a
        conspiracy—like on *The X-Files* Roswell–style!

JAY'S DELUSION: *We enter into* JAY'S HEAD *and see* . . .

INT. LAB—DAY

We PAN *over from a chimp in a chemist's coat measuring liquids in a
pair of beekers to a chimp at a drafting table sketching blueprints for an
insidious war machine. An orangutan shakes hands with a group of five
well-dressed men, one of which looks like the Cigarette Smoking Man
from* The X-Files.

                                  JAY (V.O.)
        Working in secret with a crew of double-dealing, nicotine-
        fiending fucks that're selling out the human race, these super-
        monkeys will use simian science and their genius IQ's to make
        man and monkey alike believe that *they're* the superior species!

EXT. BALCONY—DAY

*A monkey dressed like Mussolini addresses a huge crowd of apes, who
wave fists in the air.*

                                  JAY (V.O.)
        Then all it'll take is one little monkey in a spiffy suit to whip the
        dumber chimps into a frenzy, until they go all ape-shit and start
        demanding more bananas, better pay, and human flesh!

EXT. FIELD—DAY

*Randal leads a pack of humans racing through a cornfield, and is shot in
the neck. He collapses, revealing a* GORILLA *on horseback holding a
rifle. Two other Gorillas throw a net over him.*

                                  JAY (V.O.)
        You'll have to be faster than Walt Flanagan's Dog to outrun the
        warrior gorillas, who hunt humans for sport, profit, and the
        occasional inter-species blow job. And if you don't wind up with
        a monkey hog in your mouth, you'll be captured, killed, or
        worse . . .

INT. LAB—DAY

Cornelius and Zera-looking chimps dissect the brain of a living, screaming Dante.

> JAY (V.O.)
> Eaten alive!

EXT. QUICK STOP—DAY

The Quick Stop is overrun by vines in a jungle–like atmosphere. Monkeys exit the store carrying bunches of bananas. The sign now reads: Ape Stop.

> JAY (V.O.)
> Then these monkey fucks'll start wearing our clothes and rebuilding the world in *their* image.

EXT. BEACH—DAY

We start on a FULL SHOT *of Jay on the beach, looking up, then* SNAP ZOOM OUT *to* REVEAL *Jay kneeling before the beach-buried Statue of Liberty, screaming, his arms raised.*

> JAY (V.O.)
> And only those who outwit those damn dirty apes'll ever remember that it was *MAN* who once ruled the earth!

> JAY
> *(at statue)*
> YOU MANIACS! DAMN YOUSE!!! GODDAMN YOUSE ALL TO HELL!!!

We DISSOLVE *from this image to:*

EXT. UTAH ROADSIDE—DAY

Another close-up of Jay's pained face. Behind him, Suzanne and Silent Bob are playing patty-cake. Jay eyes Suzanne angrily.

> JAY
> Not on my watch, motherfucker!

Jay turns and rushes Suzanne, ferociously.

JAY
DIE, YOU SUPER-MONKEY FUCK! DIE!!!

Jay trips on a root poking out of the ground and hits the dirt. Suzanne then goes over to Jay, pulls his face to hers, and kisses him on the lips.

JAY
Alright—you can live. For now.

Silent Bob helps Jay to his feet.

JAY
You see that? Bitches love me.
(heading off)
C'mon—let's get something to eat.

Bob stops Jay and points at Suzanne, protesting.

JAY
I ain't hiding out in the fucking woods no more. We gotta get to Hollywood, remember?
(heading off)
Besides—we're in the fucking clear, yo. It's not like anyone knows *we* stole the monkey.

INT. TV NEWS STATION—DAY

An ANCHORMAN *addresses the camera.*

ANCHORMAN
I'm Reg Hartner and this is a News Now Bulletin. A Provasik animal testing facility in Boulder was the focus of an attack by a terroristic primate rescue syndicate calling themselves the Coalition for Liberation of Itinerant Tree-dwellers. Or simply, C.L.I.T.

A graphic of the C.L.I.T. *logo appears beside him, nailing home the joke.*

ANCHORMAN
In a videotape sent to authorities this morning, credit for the liberation of an orangutan from the lab last night is taken by these men . . .

A VIDEO CAPTURE *of* JAY *and* SILENT BOB *from prebreak-in appears on screen.*

> ANCHORMAN
> . . . identified in literature that accompanied the tape as Jay and Silent Bob. In this chilling clip, they make it very clear that they are in control of the C.L.I.T.

On screen is the C.L.I.T. *Logo. A digitized voice narrates.*

> DIGITIZED VOICE
> We are the C.L.I.T. None of you are safe. Now tremble before the might of our merciless leader.

The logo gives way to the video of Jay and Bob that Sissy shot before the Provasik break-in. Jay's yelling into the camera.

> JAY
> I AM THE CLIT COMMANDER!!!

Coming out of the video footage, the Anchorman shakes his head, chilled.

> ANCHORMAN
> Terrifying. Here to help us understand this footage is Federal Wildlife Marshal Willenholly.

PULL OUT *to reveal Willenholly beside the Anchorman.*

> ANCHORMAN
> Marshal, what can you tell us about the C.L.I.T.?

> WILLENHOLLY
> From the intelligence we've been able to gather, we've discovered that the C.L.I.T. is a tiny offshoot of the L.A.B.I.A.

> ANCHORMAN
> The Liberate Apes Before Imprisoning Apes movement.

> WILLENHOLLY
> Exactly. The men you saw in the video are believed to be the masterminds responsible for the frenzied C.L.I.T. activity last night. They go by the obvious code names "Jay" and "Silent Bob."
>
> *(to camera)*

If you should come across them or *any* other C.L.I.T.-ies,
please—exercise extreme caution.

INT. POTZER'S INC. OFFICE—NIGHT

On the TV screen is Willenholly and the video capture of Jay and Silent Bob. Holden looks up from his drawing table, shocked.

> ANCHORMAN (O.C.)
> *(from TV)*
> Marshal, how do you respond to allegations that the Federal Wildlife Marshal's Office allowed the C.L.I.T. to slip through their fingers?

> WILLENHOLLY (O.C.)
> Nonsense. We're all over the C.L.I.T., Reg.

> HOLDEN
> *(shakes his head)*
> Nights like this, I miss dating a lesbian.

INT. QUICK STOP—NIGHT

From behind the register, Dante and Randal stare at the TV, slack-jawed.

> ANCHORMAN (O.C.)
> *(from TV)*
> Is there also speculation that Jay and Silent Bob may be responsible for the Diamond Exchange jewel heist that occurred in the same vicinity of downtown Boulder last night?

> WILLENHOLLY (O.C.)
> There's nothing to suggest that, no. But these men are still to be considered very dangerous.

> RANDAL
> *(to Dante)*
> I told you that restraining order was a good idea.

EXT. SEEDY MOTEL ROOMS—SAME

On the second-floor terrace of a run-down, roadside motel, Sissy, Missy, and Chrissy dance in their undies and drink champagne. On the first-floor terrace below, Justice leans against the open sliding glass door, watching the news report on a TV inside the room with the volume turned way up.

ANCHORMAN
(on TV)

Is that your cell phone?

WILLENHOLLY
(on TV)

Yes. Excuse me.
(on TV; into cell phone)
Federal Wildlife Marshal. I'm on my way!
(shuts phone; to anchorman)
We got 'em. They're in Utah.
(to camera)
Citizens of Utah—steer clear of the C.L.I.T. Stimulation of the C.L.I.T. is *not* recommended.

SISSY
(yelling down)

It is in *this* house, mister.

Justice turns the TV off and yells up to Sissy.

JUSTICE

Your tape worked. The news is all about Jay and Bob's Provasik break-in, with almost no mention of the Diamond heist.

SISSY
(yelling down to Justice)

I told you those two were the perfect patsies. Now we lay low for awhile—just in case—and start planning the next job.

JUSTICE

Don't you feel any regret? Jay and Bob don't deserve this. They were really sweet.

CHRISSY

The only thing I regret is not gutting that little trout-mouth prick like a fish and playing Twister with his vitals.

MISSY

You are *so* nasty.

CHRISSY
(playful)
I'll show you nasty, you little slut.

SISSY
Would you two get a room?

CHRISSY
Fine—we'll take yours.
(getting up in Sissy's face)
I am gonna stain your sheets, bi-otch.

Chrissy dances away with Missy, heading inside. Sissy rolls her eyes.

SISSY
Sarah Lawrence girls. Go figure.

JUSTICE
They're *your* gang.

SISSY
Oh, and not yours? You know, I don't get you, Justice. You used
to be all about the girl stuff: stealing, boning, blowing shit up.
Now you're like this little priss with a conscience. It's really a
fucking drag.

JUSTICE
We all gotta grow up some time.

SISSY
If moping around over some little boy you're crushing on is being
grown-up, then pass me my Wonder Woman underoos.

JUSTICE
Don't you feel the least bit of guilt for what we did to those guys?

SISSY
Awww. Does Jussy-wussy feel all dirty about setting up her
boyfriend? Then how about taking a shower?

*Sissy dumps the bag of diamonds over the side of the terrace. They rain
down on Justice below. Just then, a* PIZZA DELIVERY GUY *approaches
the lower terrace, carrying a stack of pizzas.*

PIZZA DELIVERY GUY
You the gals that ordered the pizzas?

SISSY
This dopey bitch ordered the large plain, but *I* could go for some hot, thick *Sicilian.*

Sissy offers the Pizza Delivery Guy a sexy wink and makes a "come hither" gesture. The Pizza Delivery Guy hands Justice the stack of pizzas.

PIZZA DELIVERY GUY
No charge, lady.

He rushes into the motel. Justice sighs, looking up at the stars.

JUSTICE
(quietly)
I'm sorry, Jay.

INT. DINER—DAY

Jay, Silent Bob, and Suzanne sit at a booth, eating. Jay chews a burger, while Silent Bob eats pancakes and Suzanne digs into a banana split.

JAY
You know, Justice died trying to save this monkey, so maybe we *should* keep her around. That way, we can honor her memory.

Silent Bob and Suzanne are oblivous, digging into their food.

JAY
Look at you Tubby Bitches. I'm waxing all sentimental, and you're all about a fucking meal and shit. Now ain't you glad we stopped to eat? And you were all piss-scared the cops'd bust us or something. You know what I say?
(singing, à la NWA)
Fuck the po-lice! Fuck! Fuck! Fuck the po-lice!

VOICE (O.C.)
(via a bullhorn)
THIS IS THE UTAH STATE POLICE! WE KNOW YOU'RE IN THERE! COME OUT WITH YOUR HANDS IN THE AIR, AND SURRENDER THE ORANGUTAN!

Jay and Bob freeze and go wide-eyed for a beat. Then . . .

>   JAY
> You think they're talking to us?

EXT. DINER—DAY

There's a few COP CARS *outside, and the* SHERIFF *is yelling at the diner through his bullhorn. Beside him are other* COPS.

>   SHERIFF
> **YOU HAVE SIXTY SECONDS TO COMPLY!**
>   *(to other COPS)*
> Fuck it. Let's give 'em thirty.

Suddenly Willenholly rushes up, dramatically ducking behind the car, gun drawn.

>   SHERIFF
> Who the hell are you?

>   WILLENHOLLY
>   *(revealing badge)*
> Federal Wildlife Marshal. Is the monkey in there?

>   SHERIFF
> The ape.

>   WILLENHOLLY
> What?

>   SHERIFF
> An orangutan's a member of the great ape family. It's not a monkey.

>   WILLENHOLLY
> Look, who's the Federal Wildlife Marshal here?
>   *(into bullhorn)*
> **JAY AND SILENT BOB, THIS IS FEDERAL WILDLIFE MARSHAL WILLENHOLLY! YOUR C.L.I.T. DOESN'T STAND A CHANCE! SURRENDER THE MONKEY IMMEDIATELY, AND YOU WON'T GET SHOT!**

INT. DINER—DAY

Jay, Suzanne, and Silent Bob peer over the top of their booth, like scared rats.

> JAY
>
> What the fuck are you waiting for? Go out there and give 'em the monkey!

Silent Bob looks to Jay, shocked.

> JAY
>
> Oh, what, man? I said that shit *before* I knew they were gonna shoot us! Yes—Jussy was a hottie, but I ain't takin' no bullet for no *monkey!*

Bob pulls Suzanne close to him, welling up with tears. Jay rolls his eyes.

> JAY
>
> Oh, brother—this is like something out of fucking *Benji!* Look man, maybe it's not that bad back at the lab! Maybe they experiment on 'em by, like, making 'em fuck a bunch of different, good-looking monkeys. We don't know! Maybe they got it real sweet!

Suzanne shakes her head "no." Bob points to her, as if she's strengthening his point.

> JAY
> *(to Suzanne)*
> You stay out of this, you weepy little chimp!
> *(looks around, thinking)*
> Fuck man, I ain't no strategist! You're the guy that makes the blueprints! I don't even have the fucking smarts of a little . . .

Jay's eyes fall on a scared FAMILY in a nearby booth. There's a little kid (around five or so), and he's wearing a hooded sweatshirt and a baseball cap.

> JAY
>
> . . . kid.

EXT. DINER—DAY

Willenholly's on the bullhorn, yelling at the diner. The Sheriff looks on.

WILLENHOLLY
**ANYONE NOT HARBORING A FUGITIVE MONKEY IN
THERE BETTER HIT THE DECK! WE'RE GOING TO
OPEN FIRE!**
(to Cops)
Everyone has bullets in their guns, right?

*Jay and Silent Bob emerge from the diner, with Suzanne between them
(they're holding her raised hands). She's now dressed up in the sweatshirt
and jeans the kid was wearing in the diner, with the baseball cap pulled
down over her face. It's a pretty piss-poor disguise.*

JAY
Don't shoot! We're just trying to take our son out of this hostile
environment!

From behind the cop car, the Sheriff looks to Willenholly.

SHERIFF
Their "son"?

WILLENHOLLY
Maybe they're one of those gay couples?

Jay seizes on the idea. Silent Bob nods fervently.

JAY
Yeah! We're gay! And this is our adopted love child! We're not
from around here! Don't make us go back to our liberal city home
with tales of prejudice and bigotry in the heart of Utah!
(whispering to Bob)
You see the shit I gotta put up with for you! Now I got this guy
thinking I'm gay!

Willenholly mulls over his options with the Sheriff.

WILLENHOLLY
Oh God, this is the last thing I need—a bunch of uppity
homosexuals shooting their mouths off in the liberal press that
the Federal Wildlife Marshal's Office persecutes gays.

SHERIFF
ARE YOU FUCKING CRAZY! THOSE TWO MAY BE GAY,
BUT THAT AIN'T THEIR SON! THAT'S THE APE!

WILLENHOLLY
You see this badge? I think I'd recognize an ape if I saw one. And
the only thing I *do* recognize here is a political fiasco I'm going
to avoid by letting this butt-fucking Brady Bunch go!

Jay is whispering to Silent Bob, still vexed by . . .

JAY
And I'll tell you another thing: what if that guy shows up around
the stores one day and starts telling everybody you and me are
poo-gilists?! How we gonna get any pussy then, hunh?

WILLENHOLLY (V.O.)
YOU ARE FREE TO LEAVE, SIRS!

*Jay and Silent Bob look at each other, shocked. They look back out at
Willenholly, who's yards away. Jay points at himself, as if to say, "Me?"*

WILLENHOLLY
(via bullhorn)
YES, YOU, SIRS.

JAY
(calling over)
So we can just go?

WILLENHOLLY
(via bullhorn)
Yes, sir . . . or ma'am. Please accept my apologies for detaining
you and your unorthodox-but-constitutionally-protected family
unit.

SHERIFF
(amazed)
Un-fucking-believable.

JAY
I'd like to offer a big gay thank-you, sir. We'll tell all our gay
friends that Utah is gay-friendly country for gays who are gay.

WILLENHOLLY

I'm sure Utah appreciates that. You might also want to make it
clear that the Federal Wildlife Marshal's Office is also pro-'mo as
well.

(winks at Sheriff)

And might I add, that's one fine-looking boy you're raising.

JAY

Well that's 'cuz he's from *my* sperm. See, I knocked up a hot
woman friend of ours who I also fuck on the side, so as not to be
all-the-way-gay. But my tubby husband here is one hundred
percent queer. He loves the cock.

WILLENHOLLY

He certainly looks insatiable.

JAY

'Bye.

WILLENHOLLY

'Bye.

*Jay, Silent Bob and Suzanne head off down the road. Willenholly and all
watch them go. The Sheriff is livid.*

WILLENHOLLY

Well, it's not *my* way—but damned, if there doesn't go one happy
family.

(balloon two)

Now, we just shoot some tear gas into that diner, and when the
two guys run out with the monkey, we'll . . .

Willenholly suddenly freezes, thinking. He looks to the Sheriff.

WILLENHOLLY

That was the them, wasn't it?

EXT. ROAD—DAY

Jay, Silent Bob and Suzanne are laughing.

JAY

I said you "love the cock"! I gotta be the craftiest motherfucker
alive!

GUNSHOTS RING OUT, and bullets whiz by the trio, who are now in full panic mode.

Willenholly and the Cops race after them, firing.

Jay, Bob, and Suzanne race away, ducking bullets.

>   JAY
>   FLEE, FAT-ASS, FLEE!!!

EXT. DAM ROAD—DAY

The trio race across what looks like a bridge (but isn't), shots still ringing out. Jay spots a manhole. He points at it, screaming.

>   JAY
>   HEAD FOR THE SEWERS!

Silent Bob pops the cover off. With bullets ricocheting all around them, Jay leaps into the manhole . . .

INT. SEWER TUNNEL

Jay lands in a sewer tunnel (like in The Fugitive). *Suzanne lands on top of him.*

>   JAY
>   Take your stinking paws off me, you damn dirty ape!
>   (yelling up)
>   YO LUNCHBOX! HURRY UP!

EXT. DAM ROAD—DAY

Bullets hitting the pavement around him, Silent Bob dives into the sewer grate as well, but . . .

INT. SEWER TUNNEL

Silent Bob gets stuck. Jay rolls his eyes.

>   JAY
>   You fat fuck.

Silent Bob struggles while Jay and Suzanne try to pull him through the hole.

                              JAY
         You just . . . *had* to . . . order . . . pancakes . . . didn't ya?

EXT. DAM ROAD—SAME

CLOSER *on the running Willenholly and Sheriff.*

                         WILLENHOLLY
            Fire a warning shot into that bulbous ass!

                            SHERIFF
               One rectal breach, coming up!

INT. SEWER TUNNEL—SAME

Jay and Suzanne pull with all their might. Bob strains.

                              JAY
            SUCK IT IN! THINK THIN! THINK THIN!!!

EXT. DAM ROAD—SAME

TIGHT *on the Sheriff, as he squints to aim.*

                            SHERIFF
       Open up and say "ahhhhh," you stoner sumbitch . . .

INT. SEWER TUNNEL—SAME

TIGHT *on Silent Bob bellowing.*

                              BOB
                AAAAAHHHHHHHHH!!!!

EXT. DAM ROAD—DAY

The Sheriff's gun fires.

INT. SEWER TUNNEL—SAME

Jay and Suzanne fall backwards, as Silent Bob pops through.

> JAY
>
> INCOMING!!!

> SILENT BOB
>
> AAAAAIIIIIIIGGGGGGHHHHHHHHH!!!

> SUZANNE
>
> OOOOOOOO!!!

EXT. DAM ROAD—DAY

The bullet ricochets off the curb, as Silent Bob's feet slip through.

INT. SEWER TUNNEL—SAME

Jay, Silent Bob, and Suzanne are in various states of collapse. Jay and Bob look up at the hole.

> JAY
>
> Just like Winnie-the-Pooh.

EXT. DAM ROAD—DAY

Willenholly and the Sheriff arrive at the manhole.

> WILLENHOLLY
>
> Wow! That was an incredibly daring escape!
> *(to Sheriff)*
> You must see that a lot, hunh?

> SHERIFF
>
> Shut up.

> WILLENHOLLY
>
> Sir, you're very taciturn.

Willenholly starts rolling up his sleeves as the Sheriff looks on.

WILLENHOLLY

You and your men stay up here. When I corner them, I'll call you
for backup.

SHERIFF

What're you doing? They're trapped. The only way they can get
out of there is right here.

WILLENHOLLY

A Federal Wildlife Marshal doesn't wait for his prey to come to
him. He comes to *it*. Or *goes* to it. Is it "comes to it" or "goes to
it"?
                    (shakes it off)
I'm going in there. I'm counting on you, Sheriff.

Willenholly embraces the Sheriff.

WILLENHOLLY

You've taught me so much.

*Willenholly then climbs into the sewer, disappearing. The Cops look at the
Sheriff for a beat, who heads O.C., saying . . .*

SHERIFF

Fuck this asshole. Let's go back to the station and get some
donuts.

INT. SEWER TUNNEL—DAY

TIGHT *on Jay, Bob, and Suzanne, looking into the distance, bathed by
natural light. We* HEAR *the loud sounds of water rushing.*

JAY

This reminds me of the night I fucked your mom, yo. One big,
wet, smelly, gaping hole, and me wishing I had a board tied to
my ass . . .

*PULL BACK to reveal Jay, Silent Bob and Suzanne standing at the
precipice of the sewer tunnel that pokes out of a DAM. Water rushes
below.*

JAY

. . . to keep from falling in.

WILLENHOLLY
PUT THE MONKEY DOWN AND YOUR HANDS UP!

Willenholly aims his gun at the trio's backs.

WILLENHOLLY
MISTERS, DO YOU WANNA GET SHOT?!?

Our heroes comply, but Jay speaks.

JAY
LOOK, MAN—SHE DOESN'T WANT TO GO BACK!
THEY'RE EXPERIMENTING ON HER!
(beat)
AND FOR THE RECORD, I AIN'T REALLY GAY!

WILLENHOLLY
I DON'T CARE!
(beat)
AND FOR THE RECORD, I KNEW THAT WASN'T REALLY
A LITTLE BOY.

JAY
SURE. FOR ONE MORE RECORD . . .
(pointing to Silent Bob)
HE LOVES THE COCK!

WILLENHOLLY
ON YOUR KNEES!

Jay and Bob face Willenholly and kneel, but Suzanne's still looking out of the dam.

JAY
See, man?! He's lining us up like fucking circus seals! Well, I'm going first—I don't want no mouthful of monkey-spit when I gotta blow this fucking G-Man.

TIGHT *on Suzanne, who's looking down at the raging water below. Her brow hardens with purpose.*

TIGHT *on Suzanne's right hand grabbing Jay's right hand.*

TIGHT *on Suzanne's left hand grabbing Bob's left hand.*

Suzanne leaps forward at us, pulling Jay and Silent Bob backwards.

JAY
GET OFFA ME!!! GET OFFA ME!!!

EXT. DAM—DAY

Suzanne leaps from the mouth of the tunnel, dragging Jay and Bob with her.

JAY AND BOB
AAAAAAIIIIIIIIGGGGGGHHHHH!!!!

INT. SEWER TUNNEL—DAY

Willenholly goes wide-eyed, holstering his gun.

WILLENHOLLY
Oh, no—think you can pull a Peter Pan on me?!

He races toward the mouth of the tunnel and leaps out as well.

WILLENHOLLY
AAAAAAAAIIIIIIGGGGGGHHHHHH!!!

EXT. DAM—DAY

As Willenholly plummets, he passes Suzanne hanging by her feet off a pipe that pokes out from beneath the mouth of the tunnel. She's hanging upside down, holding Jay and Silent Bob's hands.

JAY
HEY LAW-DOG! SEE YOU IN HELL, COCK-SMOKER!!!

EXT. DAM BOTTOM—DAY

Willenholly plummets toward the water below and ker-splashes into the drink.

EXT. DAM—DAY

Suzanne has pulled Jay and Silent Bob back into the mouth of the tunnel.

JAY
You see that shit? Damn—remind me not to get on the monkey's bad side. Yo—boost her up, so we can get the fuck out of here.

Silent Bob lifts Suzanne over the tunnel onto the . . .

EXT. DAM ROAD—DAY

. . . pavement near the manhole. She sits there, looking down.

EXT. DAM—DAY

Silent Bob lifts Jay over the top of the tunnel toward the road.

EXT. DAM ROAD—DAY

Suzanne sits by the side of the road. A car pulls into the shot.

Jay and Silent Bob climb over the cliff onto the highway just in time to see . . .

The passenger door slamming on a TRUCK *with Los Angeles plates and a sign that reads:* CRITTERS OF HOLLYWOOD. *Suzanne is looking out the back window, waving.*

Jay and Bob leap to their feet, chasing after the truck.

> JAY
> HEY! GET THE FUCK OFF HER, MAN! THAT'S MY EX-GIRLFRIEND'S MONKEY!!!

The truck speeds away in the distance. Jay and Silent Bob stand there, panting.

> JAY
> Man! Who the fuck just steals a monkey?!

Silent Bob indicates themselves.

> JAY
> Oh yeah.
> *(pissed)*
> Well this fucking blows! We got one more day to stop those fucks from making that movie, and someone goes and takes the only thing I had left from the one woman I ever loved enough *NOT* to try to stick my hand down her pants!

Silent Bob mimes that they should go after Suzanne.

                    JAY
Go after the monkey? How the fuck are we supposed to know
where that thing's going?

Silent Bob mimes in the direction the car went. Jay stares at him.

                    JAY
What? What is that supposed to mean?! Don't just fucking point,
like . . .
              (imitates him)
You ain't the broad in *Children of a Lesser God*. Use your fucking
mouth for more than eating, ya tubby bitch!

Bob starts an elaborate pantomime. Jay tries to guess what he's saying.

                    JAY
You gotta take a shit? No—you gotta take a salad? Take a salad?
What the fuck are you trying to say?

Silent Bob grows frustrated, continuing his pantomime. Jay hits him.

                    JAY
Just *say* it instead of making me aks twenty fucking questions!
How come you can always tell that stupid Amy story, but you
can't spit out something like, "Yo—I disagree with you, Jay," or,
"These are good cheese-fries."

Bob's on the verge of tears, trying to mime out his message.

                    JAY
JUST FUCKING SAY IT ALREADY?!?

Silent Bob grabs Jay and screams into his face.

                 SILENT BOB
THE SIGN ON THE BACK OF THE CAR SAID CRITTERS OF
HOLLYWOOD, YOU DUMB FUCK!!!

Bob releases Jay, breathing heavily, and storms off in the direction the car went. Jay watches him go for a beat, then follows, muttering under his breath . . .

JAY

Say it, don't spray it, bitch.

EXT. SHERIFF'S OFFICE—DAY

An ESTABLISHING SHOT.

SHERIFF (O.C.)

"And might I add, that's one fine-looking boy you're raising."

INT. SHERIFF'S OFFICE—DAY

The Sheriff and his men stand around, eating donuts, laughing. The Station doors slam open, and Willenholly enters, soaking wet. All the Cops stare at him.

SHERIFF

Well, if it isn't the wildlife expert. Did you come to it or go to it?

WILLENHOLLY

Do you have a microwave here, Sheriff?

SHERIFF

We have a toaster oven. Why?

WILLHOLLY

Because I need to dry my gun out so I can SHOOT YOU WITH IT! TWICE!

SHERIFF

This might cheer you up.
(hands him paper)
Your office just faxed this over. Guy there says it's a post from an Internet chat board, signed by a "Jay and Silent Bob." Your man thinks it's a lead as to where those fellas are taking the ape.

WILLENHOLLY
(reading)
"All you motherfuckers are gonna pay. You are the ones who are

ball-lickers. We're gonna fuck your mothers while you watch and cry like little bitches. Once we get to Hollywood . . ."

> *(looks up)*

They're going to Hollywood.

EXT. HOLLYWOOD—MONTAGE

We take a quick visual tour of the city, including the sign, the line in front of Krispy Kreme, the line in front of Coffee Bean and Tea Leaf, the Simpsons *star on the Walk-of-Fame, the Rocky and Bullwinkle statue, the Beverly Center, Jerry's Famous Deli, the Hollywood and Vine sign, Mann's Chinese Theater, the* Star Wars *footprints outside of Mann's, the Chateau Marmont, people on cell phones, Trashy Lingerie, HOOKERS propositioning a potential JOHN, and finally . . .*

EXT. HOLLYWOOD BLVD.—DAY

We start on the street sign, and PAN DOWN to a JEEP WRANGLER that pulls up. A gorgeous WOMAN in sunglasses drives, with Silent Bob sitting in the back seat. After a beat, Jay pops up from under the dash, wiping his mouth, looking around. The Woman sighs, and zips up her pants. Jay and Bob hop out and wave to the Woman as the car pulls away. Bob offers Jay a look.

JAY

What? It's not like it's cheating. Justice blew up.

Two HOOKERS approach them.

HOOKER 1

Hey, little man. You want some of this?

HOOKER 2

How about you, Big Boy?

HOOKER 1

If you've got fifty bucks, we can get *nasty.*

JAY

Oh yeah? How nasty?

HOOKER 2

As nasty as you wanna be, poppie.

JAY

Alright—first, I'll want to tongue your bung while you juggle my balls in one hand and play with my asshole with the other. But don't stick your finger in. Then, I'll wanna pinky you and put it in your friend's brown, while Silent Bob spanks into a Dixie cup. After that, I'll wanna smell your titties for a while, and you can pull my nutsack up over my dick, so it looks like a Bullfrog. Then, I want you to flick at my nuts while your friend spanks me into the same Dixie cup Silent Bob jizzed in. Then we throw the Dixie cup out.

The Hookers look at him, dumbfounded. Then . . .

HOOKER 1

Oh, that's it, honey. I quit.
                  (walking away)
This job just passed the point of no return.

HOOKER 2

                  (to Jay)
You one fucked up puppy, poppie.

JAY

                  (watching them go)
What?! You said 'nasty'!
                  (shakes his head; to Bob)
Man, chicks in Hollywood are so stuck up.

EXT. HOLLYWOOD BLVD.—LATER

Jay and Silent Bob walk.

JAY

Alright, here's the plan: first, we find out where they're shooting that movie at. After we shut that shit down, we can start looking for the monkey. But before we do any of that shit, we gotta find a motherfucker in the know. Someone who's like, the mayor of Hollywood.

They pass a DEALER *leaning against a wall, trying to make a sale.*

DEALER

                  (subtly)
Crack? You want some crack? Sweet-ass rock. Get you high.

JAY

No, man. But you want some weed?

DEALER
(beat)

You on the job?

JAY
(pulling out a card)
Yeah, boy. Jersey Local 408.

CLOSE ON THE CARD. *It reads:* UNITED JERSEY BROTHERHOOD OF DEALERS, LOCAL 408. *There's a graphic of a stoner beside it.*

DEALER

I'm Los Angeles Local 305!

They shake hands, slapping each other on the back like Union brothers.

DEALER

You guys got medical in Jersey yet?

JAY

Shit, no. We might have to strike in September.

DEALER

Norma Rae like a motherfucker. You gots to get your benefits, you know what I'm saying?

JAY

I hear that. Yo—maybe you can help us out. You know where they're shooting a movie around here?

DEALER

You in this town and you gonna ask that question? Be a little more specific.

JAY

It's a Miramax flick. We gotta bust it up so people stop calling us names on the Internet, even though they're not really talking about *us* but these characters *based on* us, and at the same time, find my ex-girlfriend-who-got-killed-in-a-car-explosion's monkey.

Jay exhales. The Dealer stares at him for a beat.

> DEALER
> I don't know what the fuck you just said, little kid. But you touched a brother's heart, so I'm gonna help you out with some directions to the studio.

> JAY
> You know where Miramax is at?

> DEALER
> Fuck, yes. Miramax accounts for seventy-eight percent of my business.

INT. E! ENTERTAINMENT NEWS—DAY

After the 'E!' news logo plays, CUT TO STEVE KMETKO *in studio.*

> STEVE KMETKO
> Is Hollywood ready for Jay and Silent Bob? A source at the Federal Wildlife Marshal's Office tells us a posting was pulled off an Internet movie chat board that was allegedly written by the two domestic terrorists themselves. It's sending a shockwave through Hollywood. Jules Asner's on the scene at Miramax Studios. Jules?

JULES ASNER *is in front of the Miramax Studios main gate.*

> JULES ASNER
> Steve, the tenor of Tinseltown is one of terror today, after the Federal Wildlife Marshal's Office learned that hot, new terrorists Jay and Silent Bob are targeting Miramax Studios for their next campaign of blood, violence, and monkey-theft. In the posting, pulled off Movie Poop Shoot.com, the gruesome twosome threatened, quote . . .
> > *(reading)*
> "Once we get to Hollywood and find those Miramax Expletive-Deleted who are making the *Bluntman and Chronic* movie, we're gonna make 'em eat our Expletive-Deleted, then Expletive-Deleted out our Expletive-Deleted, then eat *their* Expletive-Deleted, which is made up of our Expletive-Deleted that we made 'em eat." Unquote. So far, we haven't been able to get a statement from anyone here at the studio.

BACK TO STEVE *in the* E! *Studio.*

> STEVE
> Jules, word has it that Ben Affleck and Matt Damon are on the
> lot, shooting a super-secret project. Have you seen them roaming
> around?

BACK TO JULES *at Miramax Studios.*

> JULES
> No, Steve. But I did see Casey Affleck buying a soda at a
> concession stand earlier.

> STEVE
> But no sign of Jay and Silent Bob?

> JULES
> None whatsoever. However, to be fair, all the feds have to work
> with is a murky videotape, so no one's even a hundred percent
> sure *what* Jay and Silent Bob look like, exactly. For all we know,
> they could already be on the lot.

*As Jules speaks, Jay and Bob walk into the frame behind her, looking up
at the studio sign. They then notice the camera and start waving behind
Jules.*

INT. SEEDY MOTEL ROOM—DAY

Justice goes wide-eyed, seeing Jay and Bob on E!. *She hops out of her
seat.*

> JUSTICE
> Oh my God! Jay! No!

Justice looks around, panicky. Her eyes fall on . . .

The diamonds, sitting atop the satchel on the table.

Justice looks at the diamonds, then the TV *screen. She thinks for a beat,
then . . .*

> JUSTICE
> Fuck it.

She pours the diamonds into the satchel, and shoves it in her pocket.

INT. SEEDY MOTEL BEDROOM—DAY

The door slowly opens in the dark bedroom, and Justice crawls to the bedside table, reaching for a set of keys. In the bed, Missy and Chrissy make out under the sheets, moaning. Sissy's banging the Pizza Delivery Guy against the vanity.
Justice grabs the keys, leaving a note in their place. As she crawls back out, we PUSH IN *on the note, which reads:* SORRY, GUYS—BUT I LOVE HIM.

EXT. SEEDY MOTEL PARKING LOT—DAY

The convertible skids out, taking off.

INT. SEEDY MOTEL HALLWAY—DAY

There's a loud scream, then Sissy, Missy, and Chrissy rush down the stairs (in varied states of undress and sheet-wrap), wiping their mouths. Sissy holds Justice's note.

> SISSY
> That bitch! That fucking, fucking bitch!!!
> *(to Girls)*
> Get dressed. We're going after her.

> CHRISSY
> Fuck that, I didn't get to cum yet.

> SISSY
> Which is more important to you: a fortune
> in diamonds or busting a nut?

Sissy and Missy race back up the stairs. Chrissy stands there still, shrugs, then digs her hand into her panties.

> SISSY (O.C.)
> Chrissy! Now!

> CHRISSY
> Fuck . . .

Chrissy races back up the stairs.

EXT. MIRAMAX STUDIOS—DAY

The 'E!' NEWS CREW *packs up. Jay and Silent Bob study the main gate. They watch the* SECURITY GUARD *approach a car that's just pulled up. The Guard checks the driver's pass, then lifts the gate to let the car through. Jay looks to Bob.*

>   JAY
>   We gotta play this just right.

Bob nods. After a beat, the pair tear-ass past the guard booth. The GUARD *leaps out of the booth, blowing a whistle and giving chase.*

EXT. STUDIO LOT—DAY

Jay and Bob race around a building toward what looks like an open alley, then smash into it, falling down. The open alley is a background painting that's being moved by some SCENICS. *Jay and Bob get up, shaking off the impact.*

>   JAY
>   I hate how fake Hollywood is.

The SECURITY GUARD *catches up to them now, grabbing them by their shoulders, spinning them around.*

>   SECURITY GUARD
>   Where do you think *you're* going?

>   JAY
>   GET OFFA ME! RAAAAAPE!!!

>   SECURITY GUARD
>   This is L.A., sir. We don't rape our suspects in custody. We just
>   beat them.
>   *(into walkie-talkie)*
>   Echo Base, I've got a ten-o-seven here: two unauthorizeds on the
>   lot. Request backup.

>   VOICE
>   *(from walkie-talkie)*
>   I thought that was a ten-eighty-two.

SECURITY GUARD
(into walkie-talkie)
No, sir—a ten-eighty-two is the code for vanishing a dead hooker
from Ben Affleck's trailer.

VOICE
(from walkie-talkie)
Oh, that Affleck. Backup on the way.

JAY
Hey! I make you a deal: this guy'll suck your dick off if you let
us go!

SECURITY GUARD
Contrary to what you believe, not *everyone* in the movie business
is gay.

JAY
Well, how about this deal: he sucks my dick while you watch and
jerk off.

*The Security Guard stops, looks around, then releases them, reaching into
his pants.*

SECURITY GUARD
Alright. But make it fast. And sexy.

Silent Bob looks at Jay, wide-eyed and scared.

JAY
Dude, it's either this or jail. And you *know* what they make you
do in jail.

*Silent Bob wells up with tears, slowly dropping to his knees, reaching for
Jay's pants. The Security Guard bends down low to watch at crotch-level.
Suddenly, Jay hammers his two fists into the Security Guard's neck,
knocking him out. Silent Bob falls into a sitting position on the ground,
relieved. Jay looks at him.*

JAY
Well what are you waiting for, bitch? Start
sucking. Bunnnggg!
(looking around)
Alright—where they shooting this movie at?

Silent Bob points behind Jay, at the SOUNDSTAGE *they're in front of. There's a* LINE OF PEOPLE *waiting at a door.*

> JAY
> Worth a shot. Like a shot in your mouth, you gay bitch. Eww, dude—you were really gonna suck my dick.

Silent Bob shakes his head "no," wide-eyed as Jay heads off. When Jay's out of frame, Silent Bob shrugs like, "Yeah—I guess I was."

EXT. SOUNDSTAGE—DAY

Jay and Bob approach the line, as an A.D. *calls out to the crowd.*

> A.D.
> Alright—bar extras. Follow me.

The A.D. *starts leading the crowd in. Jay and Bob blend in and follow inside.*

EXT. HIGHWAY—DAY

An official-looking car tears down the road.

INT. CAR—SAME

Willenholly drives, dialing his cell phone.

> PHONE VOICE
> Federal Bureau of Investigation.

> WILLENHOLLY
> Yes, this is Federal Wildlife Marshal Willenholly. Can I speak with Agent Sid Enmarty, please?

> PHONE VOICE
> One moment, please.

INT. AGENT ENMARTY'S OFFICE—SAME

AGENT SID ENMARTY *works at his desk.*

> SPEAKER VOICE
> Agent Enmarty? A Marshal Willenholly calling.

AGENT SID
(perking up)
Holy shit! Yeah, put him through.
(calling off)
YO! INCOMING BITCH BOY PHONER!

Two other AGENTS *rush in, chuckling. All gather around the phone as Sid presses the speaker button.*

AGENT SID
Willenholly?

BEGIN CROSS-CUTTING WITH WILLENHOLLY:

WILLENHOLLY
Sid? Hey, buddy. I'm calling because I could really use your help on this killer case I'm working.

AGENT SID
I'll bet, Will. What's it this time? Beaver trouble? Some kind of unauthorized marsupial trafficking?

The Agents crack up, stifling their laughter.

WILLENHOLLY
(taking it in stride)
No, no—nothing like that. Say—there aren't other people listening in, are there?

AGENT SID
No way, man. It's just me and you talking here.

WILLENHOLLY
Good. I'm tracking a monkey down that's on its way to Los Angeles, and I could sure use some bureau backup.

AGENT SID
Los Angeles, hunh? Maybe we should stake out Clint Eastwood's place. Didn't he used to drive around with a monkey that'd punch people and drink beer?

The Agents crack up. Willenholly's catching on.

                              WILLENHOLLY
                Am, uh . . . Am I on speaker phone?

                              AGENT SID
                No way . . . *Dunston!*

                              WILLENHOLLY
                Alright, now that's not fair. I know I didn't make it as high up as
                you guys, but my job's just as important.

                              AGENT SID
                Calm down, Will. Don't go all . . . *bananas* on us!

The Agents crack up even more. Willenholly's pissed.

                              WILLENHOLLY
                I come to you as a friend—as a fellow professional—and this is
                the shit I get?!

                              AGENT SID
                You're right, Will. Tell you what—we'll get our best man on your
                case right away. You might've heard of him. He's a doctor.

                              WILLENHOLLY
                               (excited)
                Oh, a doctor?

                              AGENT SID
                His name's *Doctor Zaius!*

*The Agents laugh hysterically, pounding the desk. Willenholly tears up,
enraged.*

                              WILLENHOLLY
                SCREW YOU GUYS!

*Willenholly throws his cell phone across the car, the mocking laughter
still emitting from it. Willenholly cries.*

EXT. MIRAMAX STUDIOS LOT—DAY

The Red Light FLASHES *outside the soundstage.*

INT. SOUNDSTAGE—SAME

Jay and Silent Bob stand amidst a line of EXTRAS. *Silent Bob looks* O.C., *goes wide-eyed, and pokes Jay, pointing* O.C. *Jay looks and sees . . .*

A COLLEGE BAR *set that looks like the College Bar from* Good Will Hunting, *complete with* CLARK *(the stuffy college jerk).* MATT DAMON *stands off to the side, loosening up for the scene.* BEN AFFLECK *calls to the* O.C. DIRECTOR.

> BEN
>
> Where are we taking it from, Gus?

GUS VAN SANT *sits off to the side, counting a stack of money. He just shrugs.*

> GUS
>
> I'm busy.

> BEN
>
> You're a true artist, Gus.

> MATT
>
> Just take it from "It's a good course."

> BEN
>
> Oh, now *you're* the director.

> MATT
>
> Hey, shove it, *Bounce*-boy. Let's remember who talked who into doing this shit in the first place. Talking me into *Dogma* was one thing, but this . . .

> BEN
>
> I'm sorry this is taking you away from whatever gay-killers-on-horses-who-like-to-play-golf-touchy-feely-flick you're supposed to be doing *this* week.

> MATT
>
> Oh—*I'm* touchy-feely? I take it you never saw *Forces of Nature*?

> BEN
>
> You're like a child. What've I been telling you? Sometimes, you've gotta do the safe picture. Sometimes, you do it for art.

Sometimes, it's the payback picture your friend says you owe him . . .

They take a beat and look at the camera. Then . . .

                    BEN
And sometimes, you go back to the well.

                    MATT
And sometimes, you do *Reindeer Games.*

                    BEN
Now that's just mean.

Jay turns excitedly to Bob.

                    JAY
This has gotta be the *Bluntman* flick, 'cause that's those two fucks from that Mork movie! Now all we gotta do is figure out a way to get close to them . . .

The A.D. grabs Jay and Bob by the arms and drags them onto the set, placing them near Ben and Matt in the scene.

                    A.D.
Just stand there and react. Don't say anything.

Bob goes a little wide-eyed. Jay smiles at him.

                    JAY
              (off A.D.'s comment)
That's pretty funny.

                    A.D.
              (calling out)
Alright, people. Lock it up. Let's go for picture.

Jay and Bob eye Ben and Matt fiercely. Ben and Matt are oblivious.

                    JAY
On the count of three, we rush those fucks and beat the shit out of 'em. 'Cause if they're all fucked up, they can't make the movie, right? Alright, then. One . . . two . . .

CLAPPER/LOADER O.C.
Good Will Hunting Two: Hunting Season.

Jay and Bob freeze and look at each other, then O.C.

The Clapper/Loader holds a clapboard in front of Ben's face. It does, indeed, read: Good Will Hunting 2: Hunting Season.

CLAPPER/LOADER
Scene sixteen, take five.

The Clapper/Loader claps the board closed and races off. Ben looks to Gus.

BEN
Action, Gus?

Gus looks up from counting his money.

GUS
Jesus, Ben—I said I'm busy.

Ben shakes his head and then starts the scene with Clark.

BEN/CHUCKIE
You should check it out, it's a good course. But, you know, frankly, I found the class rather elementary.

CLARK
You know, I don't doubt that it was. I remember that class. It was just between recess and lunch.

BEN/CHUCKIE
Are we gonna have a problem again?

CLARK
There's no problem. I was still just hoping you might give me some insight into the evolution of the market economy in the Southern Colonies. See, Wood says . . .

MATT/WILL
(stepping in)
What'd I say? Didn't I say you'd be back here regurgitating Gordon Wood. But you forgot about Vickers . . .

CLARK

No, I just *read* Vickers, so I'm up on inherited wealth, Hunting. But you're not the angry, brilliant young mind you once were, just itching to vent your frustrations.

In the background, Jay and Silent Bob get bored and head out of the shot. After a beat, they get pushed back in by the A.D.

CLARK

Once Sean told you it wasn't your fault, you lost the edge, William. You stopped hitting the books with a vengeance, and now I've read shit you haven't even heard about yet. Face facts, my friend—love made you a soft little pussy-boy, unable to stand up to an academic showdown, like you used to. You're just no longer that *good*—Will Hunting.
(gets in his face)
Now how do you like *them* apples?

Matt/Will turns away angrily, facing Ben/Chuckie, looking downwards, steaming.

BEN/CHUCKIE

I don't like the sound of them apples, Will. What're we gonna do now?

MATT/WILL

Chuckie . . .
(snarling)
It's Hunting season.

Matt/Will spins to face Clark with two huge guns in his hands. He blows Clark away. Jay and Bob hit the deck. Matt/Will stands there, guns smoking.

BEN/CHUCKIE

Apple sauce, bitch.

Suddenly, the door to the soundstage swings open, and the Security Guard Jay knocked out rushes in, followed by other SECURITY GUARDS who comb the place.

SECURITY GUARD

Sorry to interrupt, sirs, but we have a ten-oh-seven on our hands.

BEN
Wait a second! I wasn't *with* any hookers today!

The Security Guard sees Jay and Bob crouched behind Ben. He points, screaming.

SECURITY GUARD
THERE THEY ARE!

Ben and Matt turn to Jay and Bob. Jay smiles.

JAY
Affleck, you're the bomb in *Phantoms*, yo.

Jay and Bob then race out-of-frame, closely followed by the Security Guards. Matt heads off, arms thrown in the air.

MATT
If anyone's looking for me, I'll be in my trailer trying to figure out how I got here from an Academy Award.

EXT. SOUNDSTAGE—DAY

Jay and Bob rush out, pulling a bench in front of the door, blocking it. They race ten feet to another soundstage across from them and head inside a door.

INT. SOUNDSTAGE—SAME

Jay and Silent Bob rush in to see . . .

WES CRAVEN *getting ready to direct a scene with a familiar-looking* GHOSTFACE KILLER, *and* SHANNEN DOHERTY. *The Clapper/ Loader's clapboard reads:* Scream 4.

CLAPPER/LOADER
Scream Four, scene thirty-seven, take one.
(claps it and rushes off)

WES CRAVEN
Action!

The Killer chases Shannen around the room, falling over stuff, until she hits him with a lamp, knocking him out.

SHANNEN DOHERTY
Alright, you bastard! Let's see who you really are!

Shannen pulls the mask off the short performer to reveal SUZANNE.

Jay and Silent Bob go wide-eyed.

SHANNEN DOHERTY
Fucking Miramax . . .
(getting up)
CUT!

Shannen heads over to Wes, holding the mask.

WES CRAVEN
Shannen, usually I say "cut."

SHANNEN DOHERTY
A monkey? Jesus, you guys aren't even *trying* anymore, are you?

WES CRAVEN
The market research suggests that people love monkeys.

Jay and Silent Bob rush in, grab Suzanne.

JAY
WE LOVE THIS MONKEY!

They rush out. Wes shrugs to Shannen.

WES CRAVEN
See?

Security Guards race through, chasing after the exited pair.

EXT. LOT—DAY

Jay and Bob race through the lot, with Bob carrying Suzanne. On a fake New York City street, another movie is shooting. The trio bob and weave through the shoot, until . . .

At the end of the alley, a set GOLF CART pulls up, and four Security Guards pile out, forming a human wall, blocking their path. Jay and Bob stop dead, looking back to see the other Security Guards gaining.

JAY

What the fuck are we gonna do?!

Just then, a P.A. on a bike pulls up nearby. He ditches the bike and grabs papers from the large hanging basket in front.

Jay and Bob look at each other, race over to the bike, and jump on, putting Suzanne in the basket. They start pedaling away furiously, closely followed by the Security Guard posse. Silent Bob peddles like mad, racing toward the Golf Cart.

JAY

PUNCH IT!!!

Bob pops a wheelie and the Bike races up the front of the vehicle, taking flight.

Below, the Security Guards stare in awe as . . .

Jay and Silent Bob atop the bike—with Suzanne in the front basket—go past a MOON *(on a billboard, on the side of a soundstage), à la* E.T.

Jay and Bob look down, then at each other. They smile. Then they look ahead and let out a scream.

The bike crashes through a window in the side of a SOUNDSTAGE BUILDING.

INT. DRESSING ROOM—DAY

The Bike lands, and Jay, Bob, and Suzanne go tumbling onto the floor, covered in glass. They look up to see . . .

JAMES VAN DER BEEK *and* JASON BIGGS *dressed as* JAY *and* SILENT BOB, *looking down at them.*

JAMES

Holy shit—that looked like it hurt.

JASON

Are you guys alright?
(*off Suzanne*)
Hey! They've got a monkey!

Jay and Bob look at their twins, then at each other.

> JAY

Yo, I think that shit just kicked in.

> JAMES

Let's get you guys on your feet.

James and Jason help Jay and Silent Bob to their feet. All stare at one another, perplexed. Then . . .

> JAY
> *(to Jason)*

Wait a second—aren't you the guy that fucked the pie?

> JASON
> *(to James)*

See man? It's never, "Hey—you were in *Loser*, or, "Dude—you rocked in *Boys and Girls.*" It always comes back to that fucking pie! I'm *haunted* by it!

> JAMES

Well, you put your dick in a pie, dude . . .

> JASON

Enough!
> *(to Jay)*

Jason Biggs.

> JAY

Yo—you really get to third base with that Russian chick like you did in the movie?

> JASON

You mean Shannon? Sadly, no.

> JAY

She's fucking hot, man. If I was you, I'd've been like . . .

Jay mimes a series of sexual maneuvers. Jason and James look on, bewildered.

                                   JAY
                          (off James's-look)
              What, man? You never did one of these?

Jay starts miming again, and suddenly stops, staring at James, blown
away.

                                   JAY
              Holy shit! You're the Dawson!

                                  JAMES
              It's James, actually. James Van Der Beek.

                                   JAY
              Yo, what's up with Pacey stealing Joey away from you? If I was
              you, I would've drowneded his ass in your Creek and shit!

                                  JAMES
              I know. Because, what—is Josh *better*-looking than me? Fuck,
              no. I mean, who on *earth* is better looking than me? I ask you.

                                   JAY
              Joey, man! She's *too* fine! Yo—did you ever get to third base with
              her?

                                  JAMES
              Well, there was this one time . . .
                          (catching himself)
              Wait a second—who *are* you guys?!

                                  JASON
              They're our stunt doubles, dumbass.
                              (to Jay)
              Right?

                                   JAY
              Of course.
                              (beat)
              Stunt doubles for what?

                                  JAMES
              The movie we start shooting in a few minutes—*Bluntman and
              Chronic Strike Back*.

                              JASON
                             (to Bob)
You're doubling me. I'm playing Bluntman, AKA Silent Bill.

                              JAMES
Bob.

                              JASON
Right. And he's playing Chronic, AKA Ray.

                              JAMES
Jay! Shit, did you even *read* the script?

                              JASON
There's a script?

Jay and Bob stare at them, blankly. Then Jay puts up his finger, indicating they should wait a minute. He gets into a huddle with Silent Bob and Suzanne.

                               JAY
These are the guys who are playing us, yo. We take *them* out, and bickety-bam! No movie.

Silent Bob nods at Jay, then Suzanne. Suzanne heads off, leaving Jay and Bob to huddle.

                              JASON
                   (off Jay and Bob; to James)
What's with the weird, gay huddle going on over there?

                              JAMES
What's gay about it? It's two guys talking in a corner. Man—why are you such a homophobe?

                              JASON
I'm not a homophobe.

                              JAMES
You are. You're always calling things gay. "Ooo—look at that gay huddle, dude!"

Suzanne approaches them.

JASON

Hey—look at the monkey.

JAMES

Next you're going to tell me the monkey's gay.

JASON

He's so cute . . .
                    (to Suzanne)
C'mere, monkey. C'mere . . .

Suzanne pulls Jason and James out of the frame.

While Jay and Silent Bob continue to huddle, the sounds of a beating are heard, O.C.

JAY

Alright, here's what we do: start swinging, and don't stop until those young Hollywood fucks are out of commission. Ready? Break!

Jay and Bob spin to face Jason and James—only to go wide-eyed. Suzanne stands atop the fallen actors, who are bloodied and beaten and knocked out cold. She holds her hands skyward, clasped like a champion.

JAY

That's one funky monkey.

Suddenly, there's a banging at the door of the dressing room.

VOICE (O.C.)

Mister Biggs? Mister Van . . . Der . . . Beek? This is Security. We've got a pair of intruders at large, and they crashed through a window we thought might be yours.

JAY

(to door; deepening voice)
Uh—yeah. They're in here.

SECURITY GUARD

Do they have you hostage? Should we call your publicists?

JAY
NO! I mean, we kicked those guys' asses bad. They're . . .
knocked out.

EXT. DRESSING ROOM—SAME

The Security Guards stand outside a door marked JAMES.

SECURITY GUARD
Great work, sirs! If you let us in, we'll take over . . .

JAY (O.C.)
(through door)
NO! Me and Jason Biggs are *naked* in here! Together!

The Security Guards look at one another.

SECURITY GUARD
Uh . . . okay. We'll just be . . . outside the door, sirs.

*The Security Guards stifle a laugh, as one makes a blow job face to the
rest.*

INT. DRESSING ROOM—DAY

Bob opens an AIR VENT *in the wall. He puts Suzanne into it and hands
her the tranquilizer gun, miming to her. She nods, and starts crawling
through the ductwork. Bob closes the vent again, and starts rifling through
a nearby closet.*

JAY
What the fuck are we gonna do?! How we gonna get out of here
without them seeing us?!

Silent Bob pulls a pair of hangered COSTUMES *from the closet, smiling.*

EXT. LOT—DAY

*The Security Guards push a cuffed Jason and James into a waiting Cop
Car. The pair are still dressed like Jay and Silent Bob.*

JAMES
YOU'VE GOT THE WRONG GUYS!

JASON

HEY! DON'T YOU RECOGNIZE ME?! I'M THE PIE-
FUCKER!

SECURITY GUARD
(to Cops)
He'll be the pie . . . in prison.

INT. SOUNDSTAGE HALLWAY—DAY

Jay and Bob creep toward a door (we don't see their outfits).

JAY

This was a good idea, Lunchbox. In these outfits we're totally
incognito.

Suddenly, an A.D. *appears, grabbing them by the shoulders.*

A.D.

Mister Biggs? Mister Van Der Beek? Great—you've changed
costumes already. Let's get you to set.
(pulling them off)
The director doesn't like to be kept waiting.

INT. SOUNDSTAGE—BLUNTCAVE SET

*It looks like the Batcave, but it's not. Off to the side, near the monitor and
chair setup, a black* DIRECTOR *eyeballs the hustling, white crew.*

DIRECTOR

Look at all these crackers. Seventy million dollars and I can't
even get a black grip?

A white P.A. *brings a cup of latte to the Director.*

P.A.

Here's your coffee, sir.

DIRECTOR
(eyes the coffee)
You spit in this? Because I *know* all you white folks are pissed off
that the studio'd entrust a multi-million-dollar movie to a brother.

                              P.A.
I didn't spit in it, sir.

                            DIRECTOR
Then taste it. Go on!

The P.A. takes the cup and sips from it. He tries to hand it back to the
Director.

                              P.A.
It's all good, sir.

                            DIRECTOR
No it *ain't* all good. Oh, you think I want it now, after your lips
touched the cup? Get the fuck off my set!

                              P.A.
You the man, sir.

                            DIRECTOR
No *you* the Man! And that's the problem!

The Director glares at the scared P.A. as he cautiously skulks off.
BANKY EDWARDS *approaches.*

                             BANKY
Uh, Chaka? Yeah, hi—I'm Banky Edwards, the creator of
Bluntman and Chronic. We met a few weeks back. I'm the
executive producer.

                       DIRECTOR/CHAKA
Oh—you're the executive producer, hunh? Well go "produce"
me a latte no white folks spit in—okay, Fucky?

                             BANKY
Banky. I just wanted you to know that I respect your work as an
artist. I'm something of an artist myself. I was the inker on the
comic book.

                             CHAKA
An inker? What, like you trace?

Banky's face drops as the A.D. joins them.

A.D.

Biggs and Van Der Beek are on the set, Chaka.

CHAKA

I don't see 'em. Where are they?
(into bullhorn)
WHERE THE FUCK ARE THE STARS OF THIS PIECE OF
SHIT?!

On the Bluntcave set, two massive doors open in the fake rock. Smoke pours in, and Jay and Silent Bob—now dressed as BLUNTMAN AND CHRONIC—step from the darkness. Jay and Bob survey the set, amazed.

JAY

This must've set 'em back a couple hundred bucks.

Chaka joins Jay and Bob on the set, looking them over.

CHAKA

Look at this shit.
(off their outfits)
A gay hood ornament, and the Color Purple.

JAY

Who the fuck are you?

CHAKA

Who the fuck am I? I'm the fucking director, is who I am. Chaka Luther King. The creator of all of this.

JAY

Wait a sec—I thought Holden and Banky created this shit.

CHAKA

And I'm stealing it. I'm taking it back for all the shit you people have stolen from us! Did you know, I came up with the idea for Sesame Street before PBS. I was going to call it N.W.P.—Niggaz with Puppets.
(beat)
Alright—enough small talk. Let's shoot.

Chaka heads back toward his monitor. Jay and Bob are confused.

JAY

Wait, wait, wait! Aren't you gonna direct us?

CHAKA

I'll be *directing* you to the food stamps line after I fire your ass,
if you talk back like that to me again!

JAY

But we don't know what we're supposed to do here. We didn't
even read the script.

CHAKA

So? Neither did I. Shit, neither did the studio.
(pointing O.C.)
Look man, it's not hard. In this scene, the bad guy breaks into the
Bluntcave. You make up some shit to say, fight him for a while, I
film it, I yell "cut," and then head back to my trailer, where I got
more white women waiting for me there than the first lifeboat off
the Titanic!
(confidentially)
They all want a part in the movie, and I got *just* the part for 'em.

Jay and Silent Bob go wide-eyed, as Chaka heads off.

CHAKA

LET'S ROLL WITH THE NEW!

A.D. (O.C.)

QUIET ON THE SET! THIS IS A TAKE!

*Chaka climbs behind his monitor. The P.A. is waiting for him with another
cup of coffee.*

P.A.

I got you another cup of coffee, sir. Spit-free.

Chaka smacks the coffee out of his hand and sits down.

*The Clapper/Loader jumps in front of the startled Jay and Bob, getting
ready. After a beat, he turns to Silent Bob.*

CLAPPER/LOADER

I just wanna say that I loved when you fucked that pie.
(calling off)
BLUNTMAN AND CHRONIC STRIKE BACK, SCENE
THIRTY-SEVEN, TAKE ONE!

The Clapper/Loader shuts the clapboard and races off. From behind the monitor, Chaka calls out . . .

CHAKA

ACTION!

Jay and Bob (as Bluntman and Chronic) look at each other for a beat. Then . . .

JAY/CHRONIC

Uh . . . Snootchie Bootchies.

Suddenly, the wall to their left explodes. Jay and Bob hit the deck. Through the smoking rubble steps COCK-KNOCKER—*the arch-nemesis of Bluntman and Chronic. He's a normal-looking man with huge, overgrown* FISTS.

JAY/CHRONIC

What the fuck?

COCK-KNOCKER

You thought I'd never find your precious Bluntcave, did you, Hemp Knight? But now you *and* your sidekick are finally in the grasp of Cock-Knocker!

JAY/CHRONIC

Why do they call you "Cock-Knocker"?

Cock-Knocker slams one of his huge fists into Jay's balls. Jay drops to his knees, wailing. Cock-Knocker then pulls a vibrator-looking device from his cape. He presses a button on it and a laser beam rises out of the vibrator, like a light saber.

COCK-KNOCKER

Any last words before I bust *your* balls, Bluntman?

Silent Bob quickly looks right, then left. His eyes fall on . . .

A wall of armaments, on which hangs a SILVER BONG, under the placard: BONG SABER—EXTREMELY EXPERIMENTAL. DO NOT USE. It's out of his reach.

Silent Bob closes his eyes, concentrating. He reaches his hand out to the Bong Saber, attempting the Jedi Mind Trick.

Suddenly, the Bong snaps from the armory into Bob's grip. The Bong Saber blasts to life and Bob strikes a defenisve pose. Bob rushes the astonished Cock-Knocker and the pair start light-saber dueling.

CHAKA
(from behind monitor)
Damn! Now that was one special effect! This picture's gonna make House Party look like House Party Two!

A.D.
Or House Party Three?

CHAKA
Shut the fuck up!

Cock-Knocker battles Bob back. He vogues some impressive blade handling, prompting Bob to make a run for it—up the ladder of the Bong Reactor and over Cock-Knocker's head. He lands behind Cock-Knocker, striking another pose. Cock-Knocker then high-kicks Bob in the face, knocking him on his ass across the floor. Cock-Knocker rushes over to deliver a saber kill-shot, when we hear . . .

JAY (O.C.)
YO—BITCH-FISTS!

Cock-Knocker turns to see . . .

Jay, standing on the rotating monitor station, holding a double-sided saber. He clicks it and TWO beams emit (à la the Darth Maul light saber in Episode One).

JAY
Call me Darth Balls. Bunngg.

Jay leaps at Cock-Knocker, wielding the double-beamed Bong Saber.

CHAKA
(from behind the monitor)
I think George Lucas is going to sue somebody . . .

EXT. SOUNDSTAGE—DAY

Willenholly's car screeches up, and Willenholly jumps out with a shotgun. He slides across the hood of the car and lands beside the flashing red light.

WILLENHOLLY
(looking around)
So, this is Hollywood?
(suddenly full of purpose)
Lights, camera, action, Jay and Silent Bob.

Willenholly cocks his shotgun and heads for the door.

INT. SOUNDSTAGE—DAY

The door bursts open, and Willenholly charges in, firing two shots O.C.

WILLENHOLLY
FREEZE, YOU TERRORIST SONSABITCHES!!!

Willenholly goes wide-eyed.

It's not the Bluntcave. We're on a different soundstage, where a kid's movie's being shot: Mooby's Grand Adventure. *There's a Barney-sized* MOOBY *surrounded by little* KIDS. *The Kids stare back at Willenholly, terrified. The Mooby suit has smoking bullet holes in it. Mooby collapses.*

WILLENHOLLY
Oh my God . . .
(to kids)
Um—sorry. That was supposed to be a warning shot. Uh—it looks like I'm on the wrong, uh . . . wrong set.

The Kids look at the fallen Mooby. One looks angrily at the O.C. Willenholly.

KID
You killed Mooby . . .
(to Kids)
LET'S GET HIM!!!

The Kids charge Willenholly, who screams like a woman as he's attacked.

INT. SOUNDSTAGE—SAME

Jay attacks Cock-Knocker with his Bong Saber, full throttle.

> ### COCK-KNOCKER
> *(breaking character)*
> You are *not* upstaging me, Van Der Beek!

Jay whacks away happily at the actor playing Cock-Knocker, backing him up onto the ladder of the Bluntcave's nuclear reactor. Cock-Knocker climbs the ladder slightly to evade the attack, dueling Jay back with the saber in his other hand.

> ### COCK-KNOCKER
> *(to O.C. Chaka)*
> CHAKA—CALL OFF DAWSON! GIVE ME A "CUT"!

On cue, Jay delivers a kill-shot to one of Cock-Knocker's huge fists, cutting it off (à la Empire).

Silent Bob joins Jay, as Jay turns off his Double-Bong Saber. Jay grins at Cock-Knocker.

> ### JAY
> Now whose balls have been busted, bitch?

Suddenly, a gun shot rings out.

All turn to see a roughed-up Willenholly, training his gun first on Jay, then Bob.

> ### WILLENHOLLY
> The C.L.I.T. stops here, Jay and Silent Bob!
> *(revealing badge; calling out)*
> Everyone stay calm. I'm a Federal Wildlife Marshal. These men are the leaders of a terrorist organization wanted for the abduction of a monkey.

> ### VOICE (O.C.)
> They didn't really steal that monkey.

All turn to see Justice approaching from the shadows. Willenholly trains his gun on her. Jay's mouth drops.

JUSTICE
It was just a diversion so we could steal these.

Justice pulls the bag of diamonds from her jacket, revealing them.

JUSTICE
And they're not the leaders of C.L.I.T. The C.L.I.T. is not real.

WILLENHOLLY
No—the clit's real. The female *orgasm* is a myth.

JUSTICE
(to Jay)
Are you guys alright?

JAY
I thought you blew up, Boo-Boo Kitty Fuck.

JUSTICE
(smiling)
You remembered.
(back to business)
It was a frame-up, Jay. Sissy, Missy, Chrissy, and I are international jewel thieves. We were setting you up as a patsy, but I couldn't go through with it, because I . . . because I love you.

JAY
Yeah? So that means you'll fuck me, right?

VOICE (O.C.)
If she does, it'll be considered necrophilia.

All turn to see Sissy, Missy, and Chrissy slinking from the shadows, guns drawn.

SISSY
Because she's gonna be one dead bitch.
(to Justice)
Hi, Jussy. We catch you at a bad time?

MISSY

You should've just let these guys go down, Jussy.

JAY

Hey, I wanted to go down, but I was waiting until I got to know her a little better. See, there was this little angel on my shoulder, and he said . . .

CHRISSY

Shut the fuck up before I shoot you where you stand in your pansy red booties.

JAY
(looking down)
Holy shit, I *am* wearing pansy red booties!
(to Bob)
Man—why the fuck didn't you tell me?

SISSY

Let's have those diamonds, Jussy.

JUSTICE

I can't do that, Sissy.

SISSY
(points her gun at Jay)
Then lover-boy gets one in the brain.

CHAKA

YO!

All turn to look at CHAKA.

CHAKA

Would any of you lovely ladies like a *private* audition to be in my movie?

Justice high-kicks the gun out of Sissy's hand.

It lands on the ground, discharging.

Then, everyone starts shooting and running for cover.

Jay and Silent Bob hurl themselves over the Bluntmobile.

Missy and Chrissy flip over a lavish, exquisitely-packed craft service table labeled CAST. *They pop back up and start firing at Willenholly. Willenholly leaps behind a barren craft service table that holds a bag of Smarties and a dented can of RC Cola. He pops up and returns fire. When both are out of bullets, they drop back down behind the table and reload. From behind his table, Willenholly yells . . .*

> WILLENHOLLY
> WHY ARE YOU SHOOTING AT ME?!? I'M JUST A
> FEDERAL WILDLIFE MARSHAL!!!

> CHRISSY
> TWO REASONS: ONE—WE'RE WALKING, TALKING BAD
> GIRL CLICHÉS!

> MISSY
> AND TWO: BECAUSE YOU'RE A MAN!

> WILLENHOLLY
> ONLY ON THE OUTSIDE!

The Girls and Willenholly both pop back up and open fire again.

Chaka ducks behind the monitor.

> CHAKA
> A shitload of white people with guns? Time to get my black ass
> out of here!

He races off, passing Justice and Sissy, who circle each other defensively, striking kung fu poses.

> SISSY
> You really let me down, Justice. Throwing it all away for a little
> stoner with bad pronunciation.

> JAY (O.C.)
> HEY!

> JUSTICE
> *(ignoring him)*
> What's it gonna be, Sissy? Which fighting style do you want me
> to kick your ass in?

                                SISSY
Are you kidding me? I taught you all your moves myself. There's
not a style you can bust that I can't defend against.

                               JUSTICE
You're no match for my "Shaolin Monk."

                                SISSY
Yeah, but I can bury you with my "Crouching Tiger."

                               JUSTICE
A little "Venus's—flytrap"?

                                SISSY
I'll counter with "Dragon Crane."

                               JUSTICE
How about a little "Bitch, My Man Ain't Yo Baby's Daddy"?

                                SISSY
                           (beat; smiles)
Bring it on.

*Justice rushes Sissy and instead of sleek kung fu, they launch into a down-
and-dirty, girl's cat-fight: hair-pulling and screaming.*

Behind the Bluntmobile, Jay and Bob watch all the action.

                                 JAY
Yo—I hope one of 'em rips the other one's shirt off and we see
some tit.

*Bob and Jay smile at each other, nodding. Banky joins them, crawling in
on his belly, covering his head.*

                               BANKY
Mister Biggs? Mister Van Der Beek? I just wanted to say hi.
I'm . . .

                                 JAY
Banky fucking Edwards! Just the motherfucker we came to see!

BANKY
(shocked)
Holy shit! What the fuck are *you* guys doing here?!

Sissy has Justice on her belly, banging her face into the floor, screeching.

Jay, Bob, and Banky continue.

BANKY
Stop the movie?! Are you crazy?!

JAY
All these assholes are calling us names on the Internet, 'cause of
this stupid movie!

BANKY
I feel for you, boys—I really do. Those Net snipers can be really
cruel. But Miramax paid me a shitload of money for *Bluntman
and Chronic*, so it occurs to me that people bad-mouthing you on
some website is none of my FUCKING CONCERN!

SILENT BOB
Oh—but I think it *is*.

Banky stares at Silent Bob, agog. Jay rolls his eyes. ,

JAY
Here we go again . . .

SILENT BOB
Shut the fuck up.
(to Banky)
We had a deal with you on the comics for likeness rights. And as
we're not only the artistic basis but also the character basis for
your intellectual property, *Bluntman and Chronic*, when said
property was optioned by Miramax Films you were legally
obliged to secure our permission to transfer the concept to another
medium. As you failed to do that, you're in breach of the original
contract—ergo, you find yourself in a very actionable position.

*Banky stares at Bob, even more agog, joined by Jay. After a beat, Jay
adds . . .*

JAY

Yeah.

Justice now has the advantage over Sissy, holding her head and kicking her in the face repeatedly, screaming.

Jay, Bob, and Banky continue their discussion.

BANKY

So, what do you guys want, to go away and take your lady friends with you?

JAY

Shitcan this movie so we don't get called names on the Internet anymore.

BANKY

Even if there's no movie, people are still free to talk shit about you on the Internet. That's what the Internet's for: slandering others anonymously. Stopping the flick isn't going to stop that!

In the background, we see Justice high-kick Sissy into the air.

JAY

Well this isn't fair! We went to Hollywood, I fell in love, we stole a monkey, we got shot at, and got punched in the motherfucking nuts! We ain't leaving empty-handed!

On cue, Sissy drops from above, landing in Jay's lap.

JAY

What's up, baby? You look *good!*

BANKY

Isn't that your girlfriend's enemy?

JAY

Oh yeah.
(pushing Sissy off him)
Get the fuck offa me, pig!

Sissy races at Justice, leaping atop her, pulling her hair.

Jay, Bob, and Banky continue.

BANKY

You guys are gonna ruin my movie career.

JAY

Well, we want something for our mental anguish.

BANKY

Tell you what: we'll settle this monetarily. I'll give you *half* of
what I made.

JAY

Half?!?

BANKY

Half's not good enough? Fine—I'll give you two-thirds of what I
made!

JAY

Fuck you—you already said half! You can't take it back!

Silent Bob rolls his eyes. Banky shakes Jay's hand.

BANKY

Done.

Justice throws Sissy off, onto the floor. Both get up, facing each other.

SISSY

Your shit is so tired, Justice!

JUSTICE

Call me Boo-Boo Kitty Fuck . . . BITCH!

Justice high-kicks Sissy and she goes flying across the stage.

*Sissy sails toward the craft service table, landing atop Missy and Chrissy,
knocking them out.*

Willenholly stands to see why the Girls stopped shooting.

WILLENHOLLY

Hello? Truce?
                    (beat)
I think I killed both of them.

Suddenly, he lets out a shriek and falls forward, revealing a tranquilizer dart in his ass, and SUZANNE *standing behind him, holding the gun up in the air.*

Justice surveys her handiwork for a beat, then calls off toward the Bluntmobile.

JUSTICE
C'mon, guys. It's over.

Jay, Bob, and Banky pop up from behind the car and join her.

JAY
Yo, I was just about to jump in there and get your back.

Then, the SOUND *of* SIRENS *rings out in the distance.*

JAY
Holy shit, the cops! We gotta get out of here!

JUSTICE
No. I'm tired of running.

Justice lifts Willenholly into a sitting position and taps his face.

JUSTICE
You awake, Marshal? Marshal?

WILLENHOLLY
(tries to move but can't)
Oh my God, I'm paralyzed. The monkey shot me in the ass and paralyzed me! Oh, the irony!

JUSTICE
(off Suzanne's gun)
You're not paralyzed. It was just a tranquilizer.

WILLENHOLLY
Jesus! Tranqued by a little monkey! My friends in the Bureau are *never* gonna let me live this down!

JUSTICE
You have friends in the F.B.I.?

WILLENHOLLY
(crying)
They all made it in, but I failed the exam. Why the hell else do
you think I became a Federal Wildlife Marshal? 'Cause I'm a
joke!

Justice looks toward the direction of the sirens, thinking. Then . . .

JUSTICE
Maybe not. I can make you a deal that'll get you into the F.B.I.,
regardless of test scores.

WILLENHOLLY
What kind of deal?

JUSTICE
You drop the charges against Jay and Silent Bob and say you
never found the ape. Make sure the world knows they're not in
control of any C.L.I.T.

JAY
Now wait a second . . .

JUSTICE
I'll explain later, Jay.
(to Willenholly)
In exchange, I'll give you the diamonds I stole, and turn in Sissy,
Missy, Chrissy, and myself. But I want a reduced sentence.

WILLENHOLLY
You'd be willing to do that?

JUSTICE
(off Jay)
For him? I'd be willing to do anything.

Justice stands and takes Jay by the hands.

JUSTICE
I'm an international jewel thief who's facing a jail sentence.

JAY
That's alright. I'm a junkie with a monkey.

JUSTICE
If I go to prison, will you wait for me?

JAY
I don't know. Will we fuck when you get out?

Justice smiles and kisses Jay passionately. The kiss should say it all, but . . .

JAY
Don't change the subject. Will we fuck when you get out?

JUSTICE
Snoogans.

Justice and Jay kiss again.

Suzanne reaches up to Silent Bob, who picks her up. She grabs his face and kisses him.

Willenholly looks to Banky.

WILLENHOLLY
Wow. There's a lot of love in the room.

BANKY
Regardless of what you may have heard, I do *not* kiss guys.

EXT. SOUNDSTAGE—LATER

Justice and Jay are still kissing, until Willenholly pulls her away and loads her into the waiting Cop Car.

WILLENHOLLY
Sorry, Justice. We've gotta go.
(*to Jay; friendly*)
Hey—stop stealing monkeys.

JAY
Fuck you.

WILLENHOLLY
Fair enough.

Willenholly closes the door behind Justice and gets in the car.

> JUSTICE
> *(to Jay)*
> Wait for me.

> JAY
> What—here?

Jay looks at Justice, confused, as the Cruiser pulls away, leaving Jay, Bob, Suzanne, and Banky. They start walking down the lot.

> BANKY
> Well, boys—you're rich in love . . .
> *(indicating Jay)*
> Well, *you're* in love. And to top that off, you've got your own monkey. What more could two guys from Jersey possibly want?

> JAY
> All those fucks to stop talking shit about us on the Internet, for starters.

> BANKY
> What do I keep telling you? There's not much you can do to stop that. Well, short of showing up at all their houses and beating the shit out of them, I guess.

Jay and Bob suddenly freeze. They look at each other and smile.

> JAY
> *(to Bob)*
> You know—with all that money we're gonna make we can buy a lotta plane tickets.

START THE JAY AND BOB KICKASS MONTAGE:

EXT. SKY—DAY

A passenger JET flies through the sky.

EXT. SUBURBAN STREET—DAY

Jay and Bob stand across the street from a house. They check the address on the big ream of paper they're carrying, nod at each other, and cross the street.

INT. HOUSE—DAY

The doorbell rings. A MOTHER *answers it to see Jay and Silent Bob standing in the doorway.*

>   MOTHER
>   Can I help you?

>   JAY
>   Yes, ma'am. Does . . .
>   *(reading off paper)*
>   William Dusky live here?

>   MOTHER
>   Yes. He's my son.

>   JAY
>   May we talk to him, please.

>   MOTHER
>   One moment.

She walks away. After a beat, a fifteen-year-old KID *comes to the door.*

>   KID
>   Yeah?

>   JAY
>   Yo—do you post as . . .
>   *(reading off paper)*
>   Magnolia-Fan on Movie Poop Shoot.com?

>   KID
>   Yeah.

>   JAY
>   And did you write: "Fuck Jay and Silent Bob. Fuck them up their
>   stupid asses."

>   KID
>   Yeah, a while ago. So?

Jay and Bob nod at each other, then grab the Kid, pull him outside, and start beating the shit out of him on his front lawn.

EXT. SKY—DAY

The passenger jet flies again, this time in the opposite direction.

EXT. SUBURBAN HOUSE—DAY

Jay and Bob knocking at another door. Another MOTHER *answers. They speak, she heads inside, and another* KID *comes to the door.*

> JAY
> On Movie Poop Shoot.com, did you say Jay and Silent Bob . . .
> *(reading off paper)*
> ". . . are fucking clown shoes. If they were real, I'd beat the shit out of them for being so stupid."

> KID
> *(chuckling)*
> Yeah.

> JAY
> Really . . .

Again, Jay and Bob pull the Kid outside and beat the shit out of him.

INT. CONVENIENCE STORE—DAY

Jay and Bob beat the shit out of a CLERK.

EXT. APARTMENT BUILDING HALLWAY—DAY

Jay and Bob beat the shit out of a WOMAN.

EXT. RECTORY—DAY

Jay and Bob beat the shit out of a PRIEST.

INT. OFFICE—DAY

Jay and Bob beat the shit out of a BUSINESSMAN.

EXT. MOVIE THEATER—NIGHT

The marquee reads: JASON BIGGS AND JAMES VAN DER BEEK *ARE* BLUNTMAN AND CHRONIC! WORLD PREMIERE!

The front doors open and the CROWD *lets out. First we see* DANTE *and* RANDAL.

                         RANDAL
         Now that was worse than *Clash of the Titans*.

                         DANTE
         I still can't believe Judy Dench played *me*.

                         RANDAL
         Hey—remind me to renew that restraining order.

                         DANTE
         Why?

                         RANDAL
         Because I'm gonna blast that flick on the Internet tonight.

STEVE-DAVE *and* WALT *exit.*

                       STEVE-DAVE
         Why can't Hollywood ever make a decent comic book movie?

                         WALT
         Tell 'em, Steve-Dave!

                       STEVE-DAVE
         Would you stop saying that?

ALYSSA *and* TRISH *come out.*

                         TRISH
         Well, that was just another paean to male adolescence and its
         refusal to grow up.

                         ALYSSA
         Yeah, sis—but it was better than *Mallrats*. At least Holden had the
         good sense to keep his name off of it.

                         TRISH
         Why wouldn't Miramax option his *other* comic instead? You
         know—the one he drew about you and him and your relationship?

ALYSSA

You mean *Chasing Amy*? That would never work as a movie.

BANKY *and* HOOPER *exit.*

BANKY

I'm so fucking embarrassed . . .

HOOPER

Honey, you should be. They took your characters and reduced them to one ninety-minute-long gay joke. It was like watching Batman and Robin again.

BANKY

Thanks. That means a lot coming from the guy who pretends to *be* Shaft as opposed to the guy who *takes* shaft.

HOOPER

I don't hear you complaining nightly. In fact, the only thing I *do* hear you say is, "Yes, Hooper! Cradle the balls and work the shaft!"

BANKY
(looking around)
Hey! Hey! What'd we say? Not in public!

A GUY *behind them calls out to Banky.*

GUY

Nice movie, you fucking Tracer!

BANKY
(recognizing him)
You . . . !

GUY

That's right, you sonovabitch! I'm back for round two!

Banky grabs the Guy by the throat and starts choking him, while Hooper tries to break them up.

WILLENHOLLY *exits with* JUSTICE *in hand- and leg cuffs and a prison uniform. They're flanked by two* ARMED PRISON GUARDS.

WILLENHOLLY
You know, I don't get out to the movies much. But I'd have to say *Bluntman and Chronic* was Blunt-tastic!

JUSTICE
Are these leg cuffs really necessary?

WILLENHOLLY
Don't make me shoot you, Justice.

And finally, Jay and Silent Bob come out.

JAY
YO! THE PARTY'S ACROSS THE STREET, FEATURING THE GREATEST BAND IN THE WORLD: MORRIS DAY AND THE TIME!!!

WHIP PAN to Morris Day and The Time on stage, performing "The Bird." During the song, Morris points to . . .

Jay and Bob, who are dancing with Suzanne and Justice (who's still in cuffs, flanked by the Guards). Jay looks to Bob, they nod at each other, and . . .

Jay and Silent Bob join Morris Day and the Time onstage, and dance us out to the coda, which reads . . .

CODA
Bluntman and Chronic Strike Back went on to make a mere 2.3 million at the box office. It was the biggest commercial failure in the history of Miramax Films.

The film was roundly drubbed as a bad idea by the denizens of the Internet chat boards, and over the course of the next year, while they waited for the Quick Stop restraining order to expire, Jay and Silent Bob tracked them all down and beat the shit out of them.

CREDITS. THEN . . .

INT. NOWHERE

A very familiar WOMAN *closes a book that's marked:* THE VIEW ASKEWNIVERSE. *She puts the book down, smiles at us, and skips off.*

THE END

Cast

IN ORDER OF APPEARANCE

Baby Bob's Mother	**Amy Noble**
Baby Silent Bob	**Harley Quinn Smith**
Baby Jay's Mother	**Ever Carradine**
Passerby	**John Willyung**
Jay	**Jason Mewes**
Silent Bob	**Kevin Smith**
Teen #1	**Jake Richardson**
Teen #2	**Nick Fellinger**
Randal	**Jeff Anderson**
Dante	**Brian Christopher O'Halloran**
Customer	**Vincent Pereira**
Cop	**Ernest O'Donnell**
Brodie and Banky	**Jason Lee**
Holden and Himself	**Ben Affleck**
Hitchhiker	**George Carlin**
Nun	**Carrie Fisher**
Guy	**Marc Blucas**
Dude	**Matthew James**
Bookish Girl	**Jane Silvia**
Beauty	**Carmen Llywellyn**
Justico	**Shannon Elizabeth**
Sissy	**Eliza Dushku**
Chrissy	**Ali Larter**
Missy	**Jennifer Schwalbach**
Brent	**Seann William Scott**
Deputy	**Dan Etheridge**
Willenholly	**Will Ferrell**
Cop #1	**Eric Winzenried**
Cop #2	**Jonathan Gordon**
Cop #3	**John Maynard**
Cop #4	**Robert H. Holtzman**
Cop #5	**Tom Dorfmeister**
Suzanne	**Tango**
Reg Hartner	**Jon Stewart**
Pizza Delivery Guy	**Joe Quesada**
Sheriff	**Judd Nelson**
Hooker #1	**Michelle Anne Johnson**

Hooker #2	**Merritt Hicks**
Drug Dealer	**Tracy Morgan**
Himself	**Steve Kmetko**
Himself	**Jules Asner**
Security Guard	**Diedrich Bader**
AD ("GWH2") and William	**Scott Mosier**
Himself	**Matt Damon**
Himself	**Gus Van Sant**
Clapper/Loader ("GWH2")	**James J. McLaughlin**
Clark	**Scott Winters**
Herself	**Shannen Doherty**
Himself	**Wes Craven**
Himself	**Jason Biggs**
Himself	**James Van Der Beek**
AD ("Bluntman & Chronic")	**Joseph D. Reitman**
Chaka	**Chris Rock**
PA	**Jamie Kennedy**
Clapper/Loader ("Bluntman & Chronic")	**Paul Dini**
Cockknocker	**Mark Hamill**
William Dusky	**Quentin Wright**
Suburban Kid	**Gregory Owen**
Receptionist	**Ralph Meyer**
Steve-Dave	**Bryan Johnson**
Walt	**Walter Flannigan**
Trish	**Renee Humphrey**
Alyssa	**Joey Lauren Adams**
Hooper	**Dwight Ewell**
God	**Alanis Morissette**
Stunt Coordinator	**Gary Jensen**
Jay's Stunt Double	**Ben P. Jensen**
Silent Bob's Stunt Double	**Matthew Anderson**
Stunts	**Charles Belardinelli, Tommy L. Bellissimo, Tony Brubaker, Hank Calia, Mike Carr, Marla Casey, Fernando Celis, Eric Chen, George Colucci, Sophia Crawford, Chad Dashnaw, Shauna Duggins, Jeannie Epper, Peter Epstein, John Gillespie, Lance Gilbert, Tim Harbert, Bob J. Havice, Steven Ito, Elizabeth Jensen, Ethan Jensen,**

Alan Liu, Ming Liu, Robin Lundin, Dennis Madalone, Hugh McAfee, Patrick McKernan, Bob Pennetta, David Phillips, Vicki Phillips, Marty Pistone, Jodi Michelle Pynn, Kevin Richey, Salvador Rose, Christopher Barry Rule, Jason Russo, Karen Sheperd, Lincoln Simonds, Mike Stone, Steve Tartallia, Fred Thorne, Mark Watters, Cal Johnson, William S. Judkins, Kay Kimler, Gary Littlejohn, Joe Withrell, Harry Wowchuk, Quinton Wright, John Zirlo

Special Musical Appearance by
Morris Day and The Time
Including
Morris E. Day, Jerome Benton, Stanley Howard, Gary Johnson, Monte Moir, Torrell Ruffin, and Ricky Smith

Crew

Production Manager	Susan McNamara
1st Assistant Director	Timothy Bird
2nd Assistant Director	Heather Grierson
2nd 2nd Assistant Director	Kourtney "Casey" Mako
Script Supervisor	Hillary Momberger
Production Coordinator	Tammy Allen
Assistant Production Coordinator	Elizabeth Shulze
Production Secretary	Zac Charles Knutson
Office Production Assistants	Scott Morgan
	Donald Erfert
Executive in Charge of Production	Kevin Hyman
Production Executive	Tracy Lee McGrath
Production and Post Production Accountant	Morgan M. Miles
1st Assistant Accountant	Lisa Dircks Carey

Payroll Accountant	Debbie Lynn Siegel
Accounting Clerk	Lisa Belen Burditte
Camera Operator	Bill Clevenger
1st Assistant Camera	Greg Luntzel
2nd Assistant Camera	Sean Moe
"B" Camera Operator	Robert Reed Altman
1st Assistants—"B" Camera	Rick Gowing
	Maricella Ramirez
2nd Assistants—"B" Camera	Kevin C. Goff
	Vincent Mata
"B" Camera/Steadicam Operator	Randy Nolen
Camera Loaders	Ulrike Lamster
	Chris Friebus
Still Photographer	Tracy Bennett
Video Assist	Thomas W. Fox
Storyboard Artist	Scott Mosier
Post Production Supervisor	Monica Hampton
1st Assistant Editor	Olof Kälström
2nd Assistant Editor	Janelle Ashley Nielson
Apprentice Editors	Jennifer F. Barin
	Ian Kornbluth
Post Production Assistants	Donald Erfert
	Alan Scher
Post Production Sound Services Provided by	Skywalker Sound, A division of Lucas Digital Ltd., Marin County, California
Re-Recording Mixers	Gary A. Rizzo
	Tom Myers
Supervising Sound Editor	Phil Benson
Sound Designer	Tom Myers
Sound Effects Editors	J.R. Grubbs
	E. Larry Oatfield
ADR Editor	Suzanne Fox
Dialogue Editors	Ewa Sztompke-Oatfield
	Richard Quinn
1st Assistant Sound Editors	Jennifer F. Barin
	Joanna Laurent

Assistant Sound Effects Editor	Christopher 'The Bear' Barrick
Assistant ADR Editor	Stuart McCowan
Foley Artists	Margie O'Malley
	Marnie Moore
Foley Recordist	Frank Rinella
Foley Mixers	Ben Conrad
Loop Group Leader	Leigh French
Mix Technician	Brandon Proctor
Re-Recordist	Ronald G. Roumas
Machine Room Operators	Sean England
	Steve Romanko
Digital Transfer	Jonathan Greber
	Christopher Barron
	Tim Burby
	John Countryman
Video Services	Edwin G. Dunkley
	John 'J.T.' Torrijos
Engineering Services	Paul Pavelka
	Steve Morris
Digital Editorial Services	David Hunter
	Brian Chumney
	Noah Katz
Client Services	Mike Lane
	Eva Napolean
	Renee Russo
	Gordon NG
	Eliza McCamey
Dolby Consultant	Dan Sperry
Music Supervisors	Randy Spendlove
	David Schulhof
Pro-Tools and Technical Engineer	Joe Privitelli
Assistant to James L. Venable	Matt McKenna
Music Orchestrated and Conducted by	Dell Hake
Additional Orchestrations by	James L. Venable
	Frank Bennett
	Don Nemitz
	Bruce Babcock
	Tim Simonec
Music Contractor	Sandy De Crescent

Music Copyists	Joann Kane Music Service
	Mark Graham
Music Editor	Mark Jan "Vordo" Wlodarkiewicz
Music Scoring Mixer	Dennis Sands
Music Scored at	Paramount Pictures
	Scoring Stage M
Scoring Administrator	Stephanie Murray
Recordist	Paul Wertheimer
Technical Engineer	Norm Dlugatch
Floorperson	Dominic Gonzales
Click Commander	Richard B. Grant
Choir Contractor	Edie Lehmann Boddicker
Choir Recorded at	Signet Sound Studios
Choir Recording Engineer	Brian Dixon
Music Mixed at	Paramount Pictures
	and Signet Sound
Music Clearance	Suzanne Coffman, Music Rightz
"Jungle Love" mixed at	Tyrell Sound Studio,
	Sausalito, CA.
"Jungle Love" Mixer	Michael Semanick
"Jungle Love" Engineer	Malcolm Fife
Visual Effects Editor	Joe Woo, Jr.
Visual Effects Assistant Editor	Michael J. Struk
Visual Effects Coordinator	Wendy Grossberg
Visual Effects Assistant	Zak Charleo Knutson
Visual Effects and Digital	Metrolight Studios, Inc.
Animation by	Digital Visual Effects
Executive Producer	Dobbie G. Schiff
Head of Production	John Follmer
CG Supervisor	Chris Ryan
VFX Producer	Celia Hallquist
2D Supervisor	So-ok Kim
Lead Compositor:	Jeremy Burns
Compositor:	Heather MacPhee
3D Lead Animator:	Jerry Well
2D and 3D Artists	Scott Mezger, Eric Ebling, Laurie
	Brugger, Ann Monn, Martine
	Tomczyk, Chris Strauss, David
	Funston, Con Pederson, Megan Omi

Matte World Digital,
Marin County, California
3D Matte Paintings

Visual Effects Supervisor	Craig Barron
Visual Effects Producer	Krystyna Demkowicz
Chief Digital Matte Artist	Christopher Evans
Digital Matte Artists	Chris Stoski
	William Mather
Chief Technical Artist	Paul Rivera
Technical Artists	Mike Root
	Todd R. Smith
3D Artists	Glenn Cotter
	Morgan Trotter
Effects Editorial	Ken Rogerson
Visual Effects Cameraman	Patrick Loungway

*Pacific Title & Art Studio
Digital Visual Effects*

Digital supervisor	Mark Freund
Lead Compositor and 3D Animator	Matt Linder
Digital Compositors	Heather Hoyland
	Chris Flynn
3D Animators	Bil Leeman
	Martin Hall
Digital Painters	Maureen Healy
	Veronica Hernandez
Visual Effects Coordinator	Garv Thorp
Visual Effects Producer	Rodney Montague

*Tiger Hare Studios/Kickstart
Productions
Visual Effects*

Visual Effects Supervisors	David Hare
	Michael Tigar
Visual Effects Executive Producer	Jason Netter
Visual Effects Producer	Susan Norkin
Digital Artists	Krista Benson, Beverly Bernacki, Brian Burks, Peter Delgado, Shana Koenig, Dani Rosen, Lynn Tigar

*Vce.com/Peter Kuran
Visual Effects*

Visual Effects Editorial	Jo Martin
Vce Administrator	Jacqueline Zeitlow
Production Coordinator	Marilyn Nave
Production Coordinator-Accounting	Susan Bendana
Production Assistant	Dana Denuzzi

Digital Compositors	Philip Carbonaro, Mike Uguccioni, Brian Smallwood, Walt Cameron

Threshold Digital Research Labs
In Association with IBM Corporation
Visual Effects

Executive Producer	Alison Savitch
Systems Administrator	Shoji Claus
Visual Effects Editorial	Ray Mupas
Visual Effects Coordinator	Korey Cauchon
Visual Effects Assistant	Aaron Thomas Spears
Effects Production Assistant	Aaron Nadler
Digital Artists	Brad Herman, Jerald Doerr, Janelle Croshaw, Malcolm Sim, Dan Weber, Lee Carlton, Bill Phillips, James Parker, Anthony Vu

Pacific Title Imaging
Scanning and Recording

Imaging Supervisor	Tom Gorey
Scanning and Recording Manager	Marc Ross
Digital Color Timer	Doug Delaney
Scanning and Recording Coordinator	Sk Nguyen
SCanning and Recording Operators	Brian Nogel
	Greg Rodin
	Briana Hamilton
	James Ross

Cinesite Digital Film Mastering by
Cinesite, Inc.

Digital Mastering Colorist	Jill Bogdanowicz
Operations Manager, Digital Mastering	Kim Covate
Location Manager	Ralph Meyer
Assistant Location Manager	William McLellan
On Set Assistant Location Manager	Javier Ramirez
Art Director	Elise Viola
Graphics Consultant	R. Scott Purcell
Set Designers	Peter Davidson
	Gregory Van Horn
Art Department Coordinator	Latifa Ouaou

Art Department Production Assistant	Jenni Desnoeé
Set Decorators	Jefferey MacIntyre
	Doug Mowat, SDSA
Leadmen	Mike R. Berman
	Alex Kirst
On-Set Dressers	Grant Sawyer
	Adrianna López-Cook
Set Dressers	Michael P. Hunter
	Mark E. Seagraves
	Bart Sullivan
	James E. Hurd, Jr.
	Roger Knight
Set Dressing Buyer	Rebecca P. Levinthal
Swing Gang	Byron Maes
	Kenneth A. Heil
	Joseph R. Pinkos
Property Mistress	Lisa De Alva
Assistant Property	Scott C. Sener
	John Harrington
Sound Mixer	Whit Norris
Boom Operator	Michael B. Davies
Additional Boom/Cable Person	Bud Raymond
Gaffer	David Morton
Best Boy Electric	Larry Pausback
CBS Best Boy Electric	James McConocha
Set Lighting Technicians	Christopher A. Cash
	Jordon J. Lapsansky
	Michael Tolochko
	Christopher Cunningham
	Sherman Fulton
Rigging Gaffer	Terry F. White
Rigging Electric Best Boy	Donald S. Lehman
Theatrical Lighting Designer	Michael Nevitt
Key Grip	Bill Andersen
Best Boy Grips	Steve Prophet
	George Papanickolas
CBS Best Boy Grip	Ron Ervin
Dolly Grip	Danny Andersen
Grips	Darrin Wilson
	Michael Stewart

Rigging Key Grip	Salvador "Chava" Monjaraz
Wardrobe supervisor	Tangi Crawford
Costumers	Martha Faye D. Sevilla
	Annie Miller
	Montana Creekmore
	Jerry Jaeger
Costume Production Assistant	Marisa Gerlach
Special Effects Provided by	Bellissimo/Belardinelli Effects
Special F/X Coordinator	Charles Belardinelli
Special F/X Co-Coordinator	Thomas L. Bellissimo
Special F/X Key	Johnny Franco III
Special F/X Technicians	Sal Rose
	Malia Thompson
Special Make-up and Creature Effects Designed and created by	Vincent J. Guastini
Special Make-up and Creature Supervisor	Vincent J. Guastini
Key Effects Coordinator	Joseph Macchia
Concept Art	Paul Abrams
Hair Fabrication and Flocking	Joanne Bloomfield
Wigs Designed and Created by	Becky Ochoa
	Max Alverez
Animatronics Supervisor	Greg Ramoundos
Animatronics Designer	Hal Miles
Key Mechanical Technician	Paul Pistore
Ape Puppeteers	Greg Romoundos
	Paul Pistore
	Thomas L. Denier, Jr.
Key Effects Artists	Michael Marino, Brent Armstrong, Mark Alfrey, Thomas L. Denier, Jr., Wayne Strong, Evan Campbell
Additional Effects Artists	Paul Pistore, Mike Rios, Jerry Constantine, John Cherevka, Heather Ambrosio
Department Head Hair	Taylor Knight
Department Head Make-up	Patricia Androff
Key Hair Stylist	Melissa Forney
Key Make-up Artist	Sue Forrest-Chambers

Additional Make-up Artist	Amy Lederman
Casting Associate	Rebecca Gushin
Extras Casting	Dixie Webster-Davis
	Tammy L. Smith
Construction Coordinator	Erich W. Schultz
General Foreman	Gregory Paul Austin
Foreman	Scott Head
Gang Boss	Anders Rundblad
Propmakers	Dave Traxler, Brian Garrett, Frank Tucker, Ray McNeely, J.K. Cook, Marc Dessornes, Kasey Dutt, Daren Smith
Lead Sculptor	Daniel R. Engle
2nd Sculptor	Georgina Johnson
Lead Welder	Osmin Romero Jr.
Toolroom Keeper	Ronald Groomes
Lead Painter	Eric Reichardt
Painter Foreman	Keith Sawyer
Gang Boss	Jimmy Garcia
Painters	Rick Tanner
	Brad Moorhead
	Frank Ramirez
Standby Painter	Alex Fleming
Lead Laborer	William J. Cook
Laborers	Edmund Acuña, William Laundis, Shane Nelse, Luis Valencia
Catering By	Hat Trick Catering
Chefs	Stan Pratt
	Paul Rathburn
Assistant Chefs	Shawn E. Duncan
	Luis Mena
	Gina Boller-Dull
Craft Service	David Kasubowski
Craft Service Assistant	Andreas Counnas
Medics	John Bocchicchio
	Gene A. French
Massage Therapist	Donald Erfert
Animals Provided By	Birds & Animals Unlimited
Animal Trainers	Michael Alexander
	Michael D. Morris, Jr.

Animal Supplier	Gary Gero
Key Set Production Assistant	Keith Jones
Set Production Assistants	Scott Brown
	Christopher Bryson
	Scott J. Helms
Projectionists	James Jeffares
	Guillermo B. Madrid
Assistant to Kevin Smith	Gail Stanley
Jay Stand in	Huey Ridwine
Silent Bob Stand In	Kevin P. Ballin
Justice Stand in	Mia Martin
Willenholly Stand In	D.P. Parker
Studio Teacher	Margaret L. Schlaifer
Transportation Coordinator	Derek Raser
Transportation Captain	Brian Moore
Drivers	Robert Brown

Paul Burlin, Tom Calzia, Ronald M. Chesney, Bill Condit, Tim Crutchfield, Michael Dawes, John D. Embry, Erin Maguire Evans, Don Feeney, Don Fratini, Scott Goudreau, David Joseph, Evan M. Kavan, Brian E. Maguire, Shannon Maguire, Steven J. Maytum, Michael L. "Bud" Ruben, Paul Schwanke, Richard F. Shafer, J.T. Thayer, Tracy Theilen, Mark Valdez, Robert L. Young Jr.

NEW JERSEY UNIT

Unit Production Manager	Jill Footlick
Production Coordinator	Lynn Appelle
2nd 2nd Assistant Director	Kristal D. Mosley
Production Secretary	Christine McAndrews
Production Assistant	Jason Pinardo
Key Set Production Assistant	Jason Ivey
Set Production Assistants	Erik Reyes
	Nora Lynch
Location Manager	Abigail Zealey Bess
Locations Assistant	Reinaldo C. Vilariño

Locations Production Assistant	Christopher Guice
Assistant Accountant	Audrey Miller
1st Assistant Camera	James R. Belletier
2nd Assistant Camera	Kris Enos
Camera Loader	Jacqueline A. Howell
Video Utility	Rico Omega Alston
Key Carpenter	Scott Anderson
Construction Grip	Duncan Spencer
Prop Master	Mike Zadrosny
Set Decorator	Barbara Pietsch
Leadman	Christine M. Sysko
Set Dressers	Jim Williams
	Charles J. Scott
	Tom West
	Michael T. Galvin
Charge Scenic	Alicia Jacobson
Scenic	Lori Marks
Sound Mixer	Whit Norris
Boom Operator	Marc-Jon Sullivan
Sound Utility	Timothia Sellers
Gaffer	David Morton
Best Boy Electrics	Thomas W. Percarpio
	George Harrington
Electricians	Will Callahan
	Todd Lichtenstein
Generator Operators	Charles E. Meere III
Key Grip	Bill Lowry
Best Boy/Dolly Grip	Tom Grunke
Grips	Bill Marshall
	Sam Burrell
	James P. Jacob
	Dmitry Kibrik
Costumer	Sherri Kohl-Owles
Costume Production Assistant	Shannon Clement
Key Hair	Roseann Diana
Make-up Artist	Hildie Ginsberg
Catering By	Coast to Coast Catering
Chef	Michael K. Reynolds
Assistant Chef	Ivan Perez

Craft Service	Timothy P. Shea
Craft Service Assistant	Doug Anderson
Extras Casting	Grant Wilfley Casting
Casting Associate	Justin Foxe
Medic	Chester Coleman
Transportation Captain	Thomas W. Leavey
Drivers	Edward Bergen, Tom W. Boggess, James D. Brown, Dennis Buonfiglio, John Crowe, Thomas Crowe, Dominick Didato, Thomas Fennimore, James V. Limone, Charles McCullough, Vincent Nebbia, Thomas Prendergast, Michael Russell Jr., William Shallock, Thomas E. Drogan, John R. Dove, Harold Wagner

---

Stage Facilities	CBS/Radford Studio Center
Lighting & Grip Equipment Suppled by	CBS Studio Center
Special Laser Effects by	Laser Media, LLC
Insurance by	Great Northern Brokerage Corp.
Banking Services by	HSBC Bank USA
Legal Services by	Sloss Law Office LLP
	John Sloss
	Jacqueline Eckhouse
	Jennifer Gaylord
Payroll Services by	Entertainment Partners
	Sessions Payroll Management, Inc.
Titles and Opticals by	Howard Anderson Company
Negative Cutting by	Viv Kim Negative Cutting
Avid Provided by	Orbit Digital
Color Timing by	Mike Milliken

"Life's Been Good"
written by Joe Walsh
performed by Joe Walsh.
used by permission of
Wow & Flutter Music (ASCAP)
courtesy of Elektra Entertainment
    Group
by arrangement with Warner Special
    Products

"Jackass"
written by Jimmy Pop
performed by Bloodhound Gang
used by permission of
Universal Music Publishing (BMI)
courtesy of Republic/Geffen Record
under license from
Universal Music Enterprises

"Tube of Wonderful"
written by David Pirner
performed by David Pirner
used by permission of
Made To Be Broken Music (ASCAP)

"Plastic Jesus"
performed by Toe Jam
courtesy of Toe Jam

"Mooby Theme Song"
written by Kevin P. Smith and
    Howard Shore
used by permission of Miramax Film
    Music,
admin. by Sony/ATV Tunes LLC
    (ASCAP)
Snoogans Music Inc. (ASCAP)
& South Fifth Avenue Publishing
    (ASCAP)
used courtesy of Miramax Film Corp.

"Tougher Than Leather"
written by RUN-D.M.C.
performed by RUN D.M.C. and
    Davy D
for Dee-Jay-Run Productions
used by permission of Protoons, Inc./
Rush Groove Music (ASCAP)
courtesy of Arista/Profile Records

"Bullets"
written & performed by Bob
    Schneider
used by permission of
Shockorama Music Publishing
    (ASCAP)
courtesy of Universal Records,
under license from
Universal Music Enterprises

"Too Much Heaven"
written by Barry Gibb, Maurice Gibb
    and Robin Gibb
performed by The Bee Gees
used by permission of
Unichappell Music Inc. (BMI)
courtesy of Polydor Records Ltd.
    (UK)
under license from
Universal Music Enterprises

"Sweet Somethings"
written by John Henry Westhead
performed by John Henry Westhead
    and John E. Keener
used by permission & courtesy of
John Henry Westhead Productions

"Hiphopper"
written by K. Ahlund, J. Ahlund, P.
Arve, Sihlberg (aka Rusiak)
performed by Thomas Rusiak
feat. Teddybears STHLM
used by permission of Universal-
MCA Music Scandinavia AB
and LED Songs
admin. by Universal-MCA Music
Pub. Inc.
a/d/o Universal Studios, Inc
courtesy of Universal Records,
under license from
Universal Music Enterprises

"Broken"
performed by Belly
written by Tonya Donelly
used by permission
Universal-Songs of Polygram, Inc
obo itself & Mercer Street Songs
& Slow Dog Music (BMI)
courtesy of Sire Records/4AD
by arrangement with Warner Special
Products

"Jungle Love"
written by Jamie Starr and Morris
Day
performed by Morris Day and The
Time
used by permission of Tlonna Music/
Emancipated Music (ASCAP)
courtesy of Morris Day
Entertainment, LLC

"Because I got High"
written by Joseph Foreman
performed by Afroman
used by permission of Publishing
Designee
courtesy of Universal Records,
under license from
Universal Music Enterprises

"Jay's Rap 2001"
written by Kevin P. Smith and James
L. Venable
performed by Jason Mewes
used by permission of
Snoogans Music Inc. (ASCAP)/
Many Faces Music (BMI)

"The Devil's Song"
written by John Wozniak
performed by Marcy Playground
used by permission of
Wozniak Publishing/
WB Music Corp (ASCAP)
courtesy of Marcy Playground

"Choked Up"
written by Ryan Adams
performed by Minibar
used by permission of
Barland Music/Bug Music (BMI)
courtesy of Universal Records.
under license from
Universal Music Enterprises

"Magic Carpet Ride"
written by John Kay
and Rushton Moreve
performed by Steppenwolf
used by permission of
Universal-Duchess Music Corp./
Kings Road Music (BMI)
courtesy of MCA Records,
under license from
Universal Music Enterprises

"Bad Medicine"
written by Jon Bon Jovi, Richie
    Sambora, Desmond Child
performed by Bon Jovi
used by Universal-Polygram
    International Publishing, Bon
    Jovi Publishing, Aggressive
    Music EMI April Music, Inc.,
    Desmobile Music (ASCAP)
courtesy of The Island Def Jam
    Music Group, under license from
    Universal Music Enterprises

"This Is Love"
written by PJ Harvey
performed by PJ Harvey
used by permission of Hothead Music
    Ltd. (PRS)/ EMI Blackwood
    Music Inc. (BMI)
courtesy of Universal-Island Records
    Ltd., under license from
    Universal Music Enterprises

"Girl From Petaluma"
written by Ronald A. Mendelsohn &
    John Carlo Dwyer
used by permission of
JRM Music (ASCAP)
courtesy of Megatrax Production
Music, Inc.

"Letter from an Occupant"
written & performed by
The New Pornographers
used by permission of
The New Pornographers (SOCAN)
courtesy of Mint Records, Inc.

"Fuck tha Police"
written by Ice Cube, M.C. Ren and
Dr. Dre, performed by Jason Mewes
used by permission of Ruthless
    Attack Muzick (ASCAP)

"Kick Some Ass"
written by Esterkyn, McDermott,
    Gueldner, Stock
performed by Stroke 9
used by permission of
King Nummy Publishing (BMI)
used courtesy of Universal Records
under license from
Universal Music Enterprises

Original Motion Picture Sountrack Album on
UNIVERSAL COMPACT DISCS AND CASSETTES

UNIVERSAL RECORDS   UMG Soundtracks

Read the Talk/Miramax Book

The Producers would like to thank:

California Film Commission
Karen Constine, Director California Film Commission
Pacific Production Services
Mr. and Mrs. Thapar and Employees of the Quick Stop
The Molly Pitcher & Oyster Point Inns
Borough of Red Bank

Stanley J. Sickles, Administrator
Red Bank Police Department
Middletown Police Department
Borough of Middletown
Rocky at Body Marks Tattoo
New Jersey Motion Picture & Television Commission, Steven Gorelick

The Director would like to thank:

God—He Who makes it all possible
Jen—She who picks up His slack with patience, love and lust
Scott—Without whom, I'm nothing
Jay—Without whom, there's no movie
Bob—For saying "Take 'em out of Jersey"
Harvey—For saying "Kevin and Scott are making a movie where?!?"
Mom and Dad—The best parents a guy ever had
Gail and Byron—A close second
Harley—For her never-ending fascination with poo-poo
Gordon—For the same
Jamie—For shooting the best looking flick we've ever made
Jim—For scoring the best looking flick we've ever made
Sloss—who coined the phrase "It's Dogma without the religion."
Raskind—who coined the phrase "I'd fire Sloss for saying that."
Affleck—Once more into the breach, dear friend
Matty—who didn't charge nearly as much as the breach guy
Lee—who did double-duty
Brian and Jeff—who did it yet again
Philbert—for sound editing advice
Vordo—for sound editing advice
Tim—who kept it all running smoothly
Laura—who kept it all running smoothly and under budget
Gooseberg—for C.G.I, there's no better man out there
Sue—for you, there are better men out there
The Cast—who elevated a bunch of dirty words with their talents
The Crew— who elevated everything else, with a smile
Bryan—who laughed at "Give me the map Scott!"
Walt—who laughs at Bryan's expense
Gina—for coming back
Monica—who makes Scott come . . . to work, you pigs. To work.
Ming—he's the deejay, I'm the rapper
Brad and Chris—they're the wheels of steel
Jim McLaughlin—the wizard of Wizard
AINT IT COOL MIKE—the Cool of Ain't It Cool
Chapman—who's merchandising my kid right into private school

Carol—who's keeping it all accounted for

Matt Wagner—for the logo we've gotten a lot of mileage out of

Oeming—for the artwork we'll milk to death

The Folks who post at WWW.VIEWASKEW.COM—for the never-ending kind words

The Folks who post at AINT-IT-COOL-NEWS.COM—for the never-ending abuse